"How, precisely, would a single mother and her entourage living in your home help you, Aleksi?"

"It would show responsibility. It would prove to the board..." He hesitated. "I thought about what you said—maybe I do need a change of attitude to win the board over. Let them see that I am settling down, that I am serious about the business of Kolovsky."

"Settling down?" she repeated flatly.

"We could say you were my fiancée. Just for a couple of months—just till I get the board's vote."

"No."

It was a definite answer, but one Aleksi refused to accept.

"No." She said it again, even shot out an incredulous laugh at his ridiculous thought process.

"Think about it." He drained his mug and walked over to her, crowding the kitchen and making her feel impossibly claustrophobic as he stood before her then leaned forward a touch to place his mug on the bench behind him. She could smell him, smell the danger of him, and in that moment Kate knew he was deadly serious—had worked with him long enough to know that Aleksi didn't make idle offers.

To know that Aleksi *always* got his way.

All about the author...
Carol Marinelli

CAROL MARINELLI finds writing a bio rather like writing her New Year's resolutions. Oh, she'd love to say that since she wrote the last one, she now goes to the gym regularly and doesn't stop for coffee, cake and gossip afterward; that she's incredibly organized, and that she writes for a few productive hours a day after tidying her immaculate house and taking a brisk walk with the dog.

The reality is Carol spends an inordinate amount of time daydreaming about dark, brooding men and exotic places (research), which doesn't leave too much time for the gym, housework or anything that comes in between. And her most productive writing hours happen to be in the middle of the night, which leaves her in a constant state of bewildered exhaustion.

Originally from England, Carol now lives in Melbourne, Australia. She adores going back to the U.K. for a visit— actually, she adores going anywhere for a visit—and constantly (expensively) strives to overcome her fear of flying. She has three gorgeous children who are growing up so fast (too fast—they've just worked out that she lies about her age!) and keep her busy with a never-ending round of homework, sports and friends coming over.

A nurse and a writer, Carol writes for the Harlequin® Presents and Medical Romance lines and is passionate about both. She loves the fast-paced, busy setting of a modern hospital, but every now and then admits it's bliss to escape to the glamorous, alluring world of her heroes and heroines in her Harlequin Presents novels. A bit like her real life actually!

Carol Marinelli

THE LAST KOLOVSKY PLAYBOY

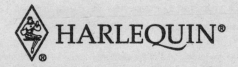 **HARLEQUIN**®

TORONTO • NEW YORK • LONDON
AMSTERDAM • PARIS • SYDNEY • HAMBURG
STOCKHOLM • ATHENS • TOKYO • MILAN • MADRID
PRAGUE • WARSAW • BUDAPEST • AUCKLAND

Recycling programs
for this product may
not exist in your area.

ISBN-13: 978-0-373-12966-9

THE LAST KOLOVSKY PLAYBOY

First North American Publication 2011

Copyright © 2010 by Carol Marinelli

THE LAST
KOLOVSKY PLAYBOY

PROLOGUE

SHE couldn't go back in there.

Or rather she couldn't go back in there like this.

Kate's heart was hammering, her face burning in a blush, and her hands were shaking as she frothed the coffee for her boss, Levander Kolovsky, and his younger half brother, Aleksi.

Never, *never,* had she reacted so violently to someone.

And, at thirty-six weeks pregnant, she certainly hadn't been expecting to today!

Aleksi Kolovsky was over from London for a working visit to the Australian head office and she had thought she'd known what to expect. After all, he had an identical twin brother, whom Kate had met, so she basically knew what he looked like and she'd heard all about his reputation with women.

It wasn't his good-looks she had reacted to, though— the House of Kolovsky head office was swarming with beauties. Kate had been petrified when the temp agency had sent her there, and she was quite sure Levander had only kept her on because she was brilliant at her job and because she *was* temporary. A permanent PA to a Kolovsky needed to be more than brilliant at her job; she needed to be stunning, and Kate was nowhere near that.

No, it was something other than Aleksi's looks that had caused this reaction.

Something else that had made her heart trip as she'd walked into Levander's office—something else that had caused her body to flood with heat as the rogue bad brother had looked up from the papers he'd been skimming through and given her a wide-eyed look.

'Should you really be here?' His voice was deep and low, with just a hint of accent, and those grey eyes with their black depths skimmed over her pregnant stomach and then back to her face.

He had a point! She was massive with child, rather than possessing a nice little bump like some of the Kolovsky maternity models, whose only indication of pregnancy was a lovely round abdomen and an extra size to their AA bra cup. No, pregnancy for Kate Taylor meant that her whole body was swollen from her breasts to her ankles. She was so obviously, uncomfortably, heavily pregnant that Aleksi was right—she really shouldn't be here.

'I'm sorry?' Kate had surprised herself with her own response. Normally she would have given him a brief, polite smile. After four months of working for the Kolovsky fashion house she was more than used to making polite small talk with the rich and famous, more than used to melting into the background, but for some reason the real Kate had answered. For some reason she hadn't been able to help but sustain a tiny tease.

'You look as if you're due any moment,' Aleksi persisted.

'Due for what?' Kate frowned, and she watched those impassive features flutter in brief panic, watched that haughty, confident expression suddenly falter as for one appalling moment Aleksi Kolovsky thought he had made the worst social gaffe—that she wasn't in fact pregnant at all!

'Due for a raise.' Levander gave a rare laugh as he watched his brother squirm. 'You've certainly earned it. Not many people can make my brother blush.'

'She *is* pregnant though?' Kate had heard Aleksi ask as she'd slipped out to make the coffee.

'What do you think?' Levander's smile lingered after Kate had left, enjoying his brother's rare moment of discomfort. 'Sadly, yes.'

'Sadly?'

'I'm trying to ignore the fact that she could give birth at any moment. This place was in chaos till Kate started, and now she's sorted everything out. I actually know where I'm supposed to be for the next few weeks, and she's great with even the most difficult client.'

'She'll be back…'

'Nope.' Levander shook his head. 'She's just a temp. She only wanted a few weeks' work. She broke up with her boyfriend and moved to Melbourne. She's just trying to get ahead, and has no intention of coming back once the baby arrives.'

That was all Levander said before their attention turned back to work, and Kate needn't have worried about Aleksi noticing her blush or shaking hands. The two men were immersed in some project when she returned with the coffee a few moments later. Aleksi's head was down, black fringe flopping forward as he skimmed through a document. He didn't even murmur thanks.

Still, for the next two weeks he came every day, and generally stopped by her desk and said hello—asked how she was getting on as they waited for Levander to return from his morning run. Sometimes he told her a little about London, where he lived, heading up the UK branch of Kolovsky, and sometimes, rarely for Aleksi, he asked a little about herself. Maybe it was because she'd never see him again, maybe because she was so bone-weary and so lonely, but Kate was honest in her replies.

She was honest, all right, Aleksi discovered.

About how petrified she was at the prospect of being a single mum, how her family were miles away, how she dreaded the hospital...

Then, on his last morning before he headed back for the UK, when there was an important meeting with Levander, his father, Ivan, and his mother, Nina, and the prospect of three hours in his parents' company was causing black rivers of bile to churn in his stomach, he found the one thing he was actually looking forward to as he stepped out of the lift was Kate's kind smile and the endless stream of coffee she'd bring to the meeting.

Instead, five feet ten inches of whippet-like flesh, a mask of make-up and a head that looked too big for its body smiled from behind the desk.

'Good morning, Mr Kolovsky, everyone's waiting for you. Can I bring you in a coffee?'

'Where's Kate?' Aleksi asked as the lollipop head blinked.

'Oh?' She frowned. 'You mean the temp... She had her baby last night.'

'What did she have?'

The lollipop shrugged, and Aleksi wondered if her clavicles might snap.

'I'm not sure. Actually, thanks for reminding me. I'll ring the hospital and find out. Levander said to arrange a gift.'

It was the longest meeting. Coffee, and then morning coffee, and then lunch at the desk—it wasn't often the three Kolovsky sons and their parents were together. Aleksi's identical twin, Iosef, had taken a day off from the hospital where he was a doctor, and they had all sat in silence as Ivan told them about his illness, his sketchy prognosis, and the necessity that no one must know.

'People get sick,' Iosef had stated. 'It's nothing to be ashamed of.'

'Kolovskys cannot be seen as weak.'

And they spoke about figures and projections, and a new line that was due for release, and the fact that Aleksi would appear at all the European fashion shows while Ivan underwent his treatment. Levander would cover Australasia.

Iosef, by then, had long since left.

Despite the gloomy subject matter, it was a meeting devoid of emotion and the coffee tasted absolutely awful.

'Shto skazeenar v ehtoy komnarteh asstoyotsar v ehtoy komnarteh.' His mother's eyes met his as Aleksi stood to leave for London. No *Have a nice trip* from her, just a cold warning that what was said in this room was to stay in the room. The trickles of bile turned into one deep dark lake and Aleksi felt sick—felt as if he were a child again, back in his bedroom with his parents standing over him, warning him not to speak of his pain, not to reveal anything, not to weep.

Kolovskys were not weak.

Levander said goodbye to him as if he were going out to the shops rather than heading to the other side of the world.

As Aleksi headed out through the plush foyer he saw a vast basket, filled with flowers, champagne and a thick, blush-pink silk Kolovsky blanket, waiting for the courier to collect it.

Kate must have had a girl.

Rarely did Aleksi question his motives, rarely did he stop for insight, and he didn't now, as he went through the gold revolving doors to the waiting car that would speed him to the airport. He went around again, stepped back into the foyer, and with a few short words at the bemused receptionist, picked up the basket. When he was seated in the back of the luxury car, he read out the address to his driver.

'I can take it in for you, sir,' his driver said as they arrived at the large, sprawling concrete jungle of a hospital.

But somehow he wanted something he could not define.

His father was dying and he was so numb he couldn't feel.

He didn't understand why he was standing at a desk asking for directions to Kate's room, didn't really stop to pause as he took the lift, was only aware that the place smelt nothing like the private wings he occasionally graced. And, yes, he was just a touch nervous as to her reaction, what her visitors might say, if he'd be intruding, but he wanted to say goodbye to her.

For Kate, the last twenty-four hours had been hell.

Twelve hours of fruitless labour, followed by an emergency Caesarean. Her daughter lay pink and pretty in her crib beside her, but Kate was the loneliest she had ever been in her life.

Her parents would be in to visit tonight, but after her

phone conversation with Craig she held out little hope that he would appear.

No, the pain of labour and surgery was nothing compared to the shame and loneliness she felt at visiting time.

She could see the curious, sympathetic stares from the other three mothers and their visitors at her unadorned bed, devoid of balloons, flowers and cards.

She was just alone and embarrassed to be seen alone.

Unwanted.

She'd asked the nurse to pull the curtains, but she'd misunderstood and had pulled them right back—exposing the bed, exposing her shame.

And then there he was.

He read her in an instant.

Read the other mothers too, saw the dart of incredulity in their eyes as he smiled over to her, as they realised that he was there to see her. Could he be...? Surely not! But then again...

'I am so sorry, darling!'

His voice had a confident ring as he strode across the drab four-bed ward, and he looked completely out of place, still in a suit, his tie pulled loose. He came over to the bed, deposited the glorious Kolovsky basket on her bedside table and looked down to where she lay.

Her face was swollen, her eyes bloodshot from the effort of pushing. Aleksi had thought women lost weight when they gave birth, but Kate seemed to have doubled in size. Her dark wavy hair was black with grease and sweat, but she gave him a half-smile and Aleksi was glad that he had come.

'Can you ever forgive me for not being there?' He said it loud enough for the others to hear.

'Stop it.' She almost giggled, but it hurt too much to laugh. 'They think you're the father.'

'Well, given that's never going to be true…' he lowered his voice and, so as not to hurt her, very gently lowered himself on the bed '…it might be fun to pretend.' He looked at her poor bloodshot eyes. 'Was it awful?'

'Hell.'

'Why all the drips?'

'I had to have surgery.' She watched him wince.

'When do you go home?'

'In a couple of days.' Kate shivered at the prospect. She couldn't even lift her baby; the thought of being completely responsible for her was overwhelming.

'That's way too soon!' Aleksi was appalled. 'I think my cousin had a Caesarean and she was in for at least a week…' He thought back to the plush private ward, the baby he had glimpsed from behind the glass wall of the nursery. He glanced into the crib, about to make a cursory polite comment, and then he actually smiled, because struggling to focus back at him was surely the cutest baby in the world. Completely bald, she had big, dark blue eyes and her mother's full pink lips.

'She's gorgeous.' He wasn't being polite; he was being honest.

'Because she's a Caesarean, apparently,' Kate said. 'I think her eyes will be brown by the time I get her home.' And then she asked him, 'Aleksi, what on earth are you doing here?'

'I'm on my way to the airport.' When she didn't look convinced he gave a shrug. 'Five hours in my parents' company and maybe I needed something different.' He stared back to the baby. 'She's awake.'

'Do you want to hold her?'

'God, no!' Aleksi said, and then he changed his mind,

because maybe he *did* need something different. 'Won't I disturb her?'

'She's awake,' Kate pointed out.

'I thought they were supposed to cry.' He knew nothing about babies, had no intention of finding out about babies, and yet he was curious to hold her—and so he did.

Big hands went into the clear bassinette and lifted the soft bundle. Kate's immediate instinct was to remind him to support her head, yet she bit on her lip and silenced the warning, because he already had, and for a stupid blind moment she wished the impossible.

Wished, from the tender way he held her baby, that somehow her baby was his too.

'My dad's sick,' he told her. It was top secret information, and he knew she could sell those words for tens of thousands, yet at that moment he was past caring. He held new life in his hands and he smelt an unfamiliar sweet fragrance. He ran a finger over a cheek he could only liken to a new kitten's paw—before it was let outside to a world that would roughen and harden it.

'I'm sorry.'

'No one's allowed to know,' Aleksi said, still looking down at the baby. 'What's she called?'

'Georgina,' Kate said.

'Georgie.' Aleksi smiled at his new friend.

'Georgina!' Kate corrected.

'I wonder if I was this cute.' Aleksi frowned. 'Imagine two of them.'

Kate rolled her eyes. Two identical Kolovskys in a crib—they'd have had the maternity ward at a standstill!

'I can't imagine you cute,' she said instead.

'Oh, I was!' Aleksi grinned. 'Iosef was the serious

one.' He put Georgina down and his grin turned to a very nice, slightly pensive smile. 'You're going to be wonderful as a mother.'

'How?' And whether it was hormones, exhaustion or just plain old fear, tears shot from her eyes as her bravery crumbled. 'I want it to be wonderful for her, but how will I manage it?'

'It will be,' Aleksi said assuredly. 'My parents had everything and they managed to completely mess us all up. You, on the other hand...' he stared into her soft brown eyes and didn't see the bloodshot whites, just tears and concern and a certain stoicism there, laced with kindness too '...are going to get it so right.' And then it was over. 'I've got to go.'

'Thank you.'

She braced herself for him to stand, tightened up her non-existent abdominal muscles as he went to stand, anticipating pain but getting something else. His arms came around her, that gorgeous face moved in and she smelt him—smelt Kolovsky cologne and something else, something male and unique that made her blush just as it had on that first day, just as she knew it always would.

'Let's leave your audience with no room for doubt.'

And then he kissed her.

Terribly, terribly tenderly—she was, after all, just twelve hours post-op—but there was this taste and this passion and this heaven that she found on his lips...this gorgeous, delicious escape that was delivered with his mouth and then the cool danger of his tongue. And to the nay-sayers on the ward he proved this wasn't a duty call.

'I have to get this flight.'

He should have been on the stage, Kate thought, because there was regret in his eyes and voice as he walked out of the ward. She lay back on the pillow, eyes closed, but basking in the glow of the curious looks from the other mothers and their oh, so plain partners.

Only she didn't get to enjoy them for very long.

Lost in a dream, still basking in the memory, she was very rudely interrupted as a porter kicked off the brakes on her bed.

'You're being moved.'

'Where?'

Oh, God—she so didn't want this. Didn't want to start again with three other mothers—or, worse, maybe she was being moved to an eight-bed ward.

'You're being upgraded.'

Five years ago, on a business flight to Singapore, her stingy boss had been overruled by ground staff and she had been invited to turn left, not right, as she stepped onto the plane.

It happened again that afternoon.

Her bed slid easily out of the public section, over the buffed tiles, and then stuck a little as it hit the soft carpets of the private wing, as if warning the porter— warning everyone—that she didn't really belong there.

But who cared?

Not the staff.

Aleksi Kolovsky had covered her for a full week.

It was bliss to move into the large double bed.

Heaven to stare at the five-star menu as Georgina was whisked to the nursery to be brought back later for feeding.

It was, Kate reflected later that night, as a *lovely* mid-wife took Georgina for the night and clicked off the light, the second nicest thing that had ever happened to her.

The first nicest thing had been his kiss.

CHAPTER ONE

It DIDN'T hurt as much as everyone said that it should.

His leg, fractured and mangled in a road accident, would, he had been told, mean six months of extensive rehabilitation—and then perhaps he might walk with an aid.

Four months to the day since the accident that had almost taken his life, Aleksi Kolovsky waded through the glittering Caribbean ocean unaided. The doctor had suggested two fifteen-minute sessions a day.

It was his third hourly session, and it was not yet midday.

Whatever he was advised to do, he did more of it.

Whatever the treatment, he headed straight for the cure.

After all, he had done this once before—under circumstances far worse than this.

He had been a child without doctors, without physios, without this stunning backdrop and the cool ocean that now soothed his aching muscles. He had rehabilitated his fractured body himself—first in the confines of his room till the bruises had faded, and then, without grimacing, without wincing, he had walked and returned to schooling. Not even his twin, Iosef, had been aware of his struggles; Aleksi had privately continued his healing behind the closed walls of his mind.

Iosef—his identical twin.

He smiled a wry smile. He had watched a show last night on the television. Well, he hadn't exactly watched it, it had been on in the background, and he had not paid it full attention. His attention had instead been on the skilled lips working on his tumescent length to raise it to its splendid glory. It had been a different attention, though. Normally he switched off, sex the balm—not any more. The television had been too loud as it spoke of telepathic bonds between twins, and the woman's sighs had been grating. Since the accident, chatter annoyed him, conversation irritated him, and last night her lips had not soothed him. He had hardened, but it had been just mechanical, an automated response that, despite her delight, had not pleased Aleksi. Though he'd yearned for relief, he had realised he wouldn't get it from her. However, there was a reputation to be upheld, so he'd shifted their position.

He'd heard her cries as he did the right thing, pleasuring her with his mouth, and then had feigned reluctance at the disturbance from his phone.

His phone buzzed regularly.

There had been no need to answer it—except last night he had chosen to. Chosen to make excuses as to why she must leave, rather than give that piece of himself to her.

Was even the escape of sex to be denied him?

The sun beat on his shoulders—his skin was brown, his body lean and toned, and he appeared a picture of health above the water. But the scars stung beneath as he stretched his limits and made himself run in the water.

Now it hurt.

It hurt like hell, but he pushed through it.

Could his brother in Australia feel this? Aleksi thought as he sliced the water and forced himself on. Was Iosef, working in an Emergency ward in Australia, suddenly sweating and gripped by pain as he went about his day?

Aleksi doubted it.

Oh, he had no animosity towards Iosef—he admired that he had broken away from the company and gone on to study medicine. Still they chatted, and met regularly. Aleksi liked him, in fact. But there was no telepathic bond, no sharing of minds, no sixth sense…

Where had the twin bond been when his father had beaten him to a pulp when he was only seven years old?

Where had the sixth sense been when a week later his brother had been allowed in to see him?

'Some fall…' Iosef had said, in Russian of course—because even in Australia the Kolovskys had spoken in Russian.

'Dad is getting you a new bike.' Iosef had come to sit on the bed, laughing and chatting, but as the mattress had indented a white bolt of pain had shot through Aleksi and he had gone to cry out. Then he had seen the warning in his mother's eyes.

'Good,' he had said instead.

There *was* no special bond Aleksi realised.

You did not ache, you did not bleed just because your brother did.

He ran faster.

Riminic, Riminic, Riminic.

Even the gulls taunted him with the name.

A brother whose existence he had denied.

A brother he had chosen to forget.

There was no end to his shame, and his leg wouldn't let him outrun it.

Sprint over, he was spent, and glad to be exhausted. Maybe now he could get some rest.

The nurse had his pills waiting when he returned to the lavish chalet, but he refused them. He drank instead a cocktail of vitamins and fresh juice and headed for his bedroom.

'I'm going to rest.'

'Would you like me to come in?' She smiled. 'To check on you?'

He growled out a refusal of her *kind* offer—could he not just recover? Could he not have some peace?

He lay on the silk sheets, the fan cooling his warm skin, yet his blood felt frozen.

The pain did not scare him—it was the damage to his mind. He had passed every test, had convinced the doctors that he was fine—could at times almost convince himself that he was—but there was a blur of memories, conversations that he could not recall, images that he could not summon, knowledge that lay buried.

The phone buzzed.

He went to turn it off.

Tired, he needed to rest.

And then he saw her name.

Kate.

Aleksi hesitated before answering. Kate was one of the reasons he was in the West Indies recovering—he had grown accustomed to her by his bedside, looked forward rather too much to her visits in the hospital and started to rely on her just a little too heavily. And Aleksi had long since chosen to rely on no-one.

'What?' His voice was curt.

'You said to tell you if...'

Her voice came to him over the phone from halfway around the world. He could hear that she was nervous and he didn't blame her. Nina would go berserk if she found out that Kate was calling. Aleksi was not to be disturbed with mundane work matters—except Aleksi had told Kate that he wanted to be disturbed.

'Tell me what, Kate?' Aleksi said. He could picture her round, kind face, and was quite sure that she was blushing. Kate blushed a lot—she was a large girl, surrounded by whip-thin models. The House of Kolovsky was a bitchy place to work at the best of times, and at the worst of times it was a snake pit—right now it was the worst of times. 'Remember, no matter what my mother says, your loyalty is to me—you are *my* PA.'

She had been his PA for over a year now. He had cajoled her into taking the position when yet another PA of his had been so stupid as to confuse sex with love. Safe in the knowledge that he would never cross the line with an overweight single mum, he had contacted her. Georgie was now nearly five years old and at school, and Kate was even bigger than before—no, there was absolutely no question of his fancying her.

'Your brother Levander…' Kate stammered. 'You know he and Millie were looking to adopt an orphan…?'

'And?'

'They went to Russia last week; they met him—their new son…'

Aleksi closed his eyes; he had feared this day would come sooner than was convenient. Levander had run the House of Kolovsky head branch in Australia. He had been sensible, and on their father's death a couple of years ago he had got out. Now he worked in London, taking over Aleksi's old role, while Aleksi had taken over the running of Kolovsky—effectively a swap.

Levander had only returned to Australia while Aleksi recuperated.

'I've heard Nina talking; *she* is going to run it...'

'Run what?'

'House of Kolovsky.' Kate gulped. 'She has these ideas...'

'Levander would never—' Aleksi started, but then again Levander now would. Since he had met Millie, since they had had Sashar, his priorities had shifted. Money had never been Levander's god. Raised in Detsky Dom, an orphanage in Russia, he had no real allegiance to the Kolovskys—Nina wasn't his mother, and with Ivan dead Aleksi knew that Levander's priorities were with his own family now—his new family, one that wanted to save a child from the hell Levander had endured.

'She has told Levander not to tell you,' Kate explained. 'That no one is to disturb you with this—that you need this time to heal.'

'The board will not pass it.'

'Nina has new plans, ideas that will generate a lot of money...'

She had stopped stammering now. Despite her shyness at times, Kate was an articulate, intelligent woman, which was why he had bent over backwards to get her on staff. She was different from all the others. Her only interest at work was *work*—which she did very capably, so she could earn the money to single-handedly raise her daughter.

'She will convince the board, and she has ideas that they like.'

'Ideas?' Aleksi snorted.

'She makes them sound attractive,' Kate said. 'I sat in on a meeting last week. She put forward a proposal from Zakahr Belenki...'

Despite the warmth of the room Aleksi felt his blood chill. 'What sort of proposal?'

'One that will benefit both Kolovsky and Belenki's charity,' Kate said. 'They are talking of a new range— bridal dresses in the Krasavitsa outlets with a percentage of profit…'

Aleksi didn't hear much more. He was aware of his racing heart, as if he were pounding his battered body through the ocean this very minute, except he was lying perfectly still on the bed. The Krasavitsa offshoot of the Kolovsky business was *his* baby—his idea, his domain. But it wasn't just that Nina was considering tampering with his baby that had Aleksi's heart hammering like this.

What was the problem with Belenki?

His mind, though Aleksi had denied it both to his family and to the doctors, *was* damaged.

Thoughts, images, and memories were a mere stretch from his grasp. He could remember the charity ball just before his accident—Belenki had flown in from Europe and had been the guest speaker, that much he remembered. And he remembered the fear he had felt at the time too. Iosef had had harsh words with him—for his poor behaviour at the ball, for talking through the speeches, which, yes, he had. Zakahr Belenki had been talking about his life in Detsky Dom, how he had chosen to live instead on the streets, about what he had done to survive there.

It had been easier to have another drink that night than to hear Zakahr's message. Levander had never really spoken of his years there, and part of Aleksi didn't want to hear it. He didn't want to hear how his half-brother had suffered so.

'Has Belenki been back to Australia?'

'No,' Kate said. 'But he has been talking daily with Nina. They are coming up with new ideas all the time.'

Why, Aleksi begged himself, did that name strike fear inside him?

He tried to pull up the man's image—yet, like so much else in his mind, it was a blur...as if it had been pixilated...like the many other shadowy areas in his mind that he must allow no one else to know about.

'Nina will run the House of Kolovsky into the ground—she cannot run it,' he declared.

'Who else is there?'

'Me,' Aleksi ground out. 'I will be back at my desk on Monday.'

'Aleksi!' Kate's voice was exasperated. 'I didn't ring for that; I just rang because you made me promise to keep you informed. It's way too soon for you to return. Look...'

She lowered her voice and he could just picture her leaning forward, picture her finger toying with a curl of her hair as she tried to come up with a solution, and despite the direness of the situation the image made him smile. The sound of her voice soothed him, and it moved him too, in the way it sometimes did—never more so than now.

'I can ring you every day...'

He stared down at the sudden, unexpected passionate reaction of his body and did not answer.

'Can you hear me, Aleksi?'

'Go on.'

'I can ring you all the time...tell you things...and then you can tell me what to do.'

He wanted to close his eyes. He wanted her to tell him things. Hell, how he wanted at this moment to tell her exactly what to do. He didn't want to think about the House of Kolovsky and his family, didn't want to face what he was trying to forget. How much nicer would it be to just lie here and let her tell him things that he wanted to hear?

'Kate...' His voice was ragged. He wanted her on a plane this minute—he wanted her here, wanted her now—but instead he forced himself to sit upright, to ignore the fire in his groin and concentrate on what was necessary. 'I'll be back on Monday. Don't tell anyone, don't act any different. Just go along with whatever Nina says.'

It wasn't her place to argue, and she didn't.

'Fine,' she said. 'Do you want me to organize—?'

'I'll sort everything out from this end,' Aleksi interrupted. 'Kate...?'

'Yes?'

'Nothing.' He clicked off the phone and tried to keep his mind on necessary business. Turned on his laptop and raced through figures. He knew only too well that the House of Kolovsky was on a collision course and that he was the only one who could stop it.

He just couldn't quite remember why.

And for the first time in ages he didn't try to. The figures he was analysing blurred in front of his eyes, so instead he clicked on company photographs—a who's who of the House of Kolovsky.

Ivan, his deceased father; Nina, his mother; Levander, his half-brother, whom his parents had conveniently forgotten about and left in an orphanage in Russia when they fled to Australia; Iosef, his twin, and his sister Annika. Then Aleksi clicked on his own image, saw his scowling, haughty face before hurriedly moving on.

Finally, for the first time in weeks he allowed himself the respite of *her* face.

Kate Taylor.

Smiling, her face round and shiny, dark hair curling under the heat of the photographer's lights, nervous at having her photo taken—though it was just a head-and-shoulders corporate shot.

He must be losing his mind.

Imagine *that* bulk on his healing thigh, he told himself, trying to calm his excited body. He tried in vain to reel in his imagination—except he just grew harder at the thought of Kate on top of him...

He had the most beautiful women on tap—warm, eager flesh on the other side of his bedroom door—yet all he could think of was that in a week he would again see Kate.

'Aleksi?' The nurse knocked, her voice low, the door opening just a fraction. 'Is there anything at all you need?'

'Not to be disturbed,' he growled, and as the door reluctantly closed he turned off the computer and lay in the darkness, willing sleep to invade. Then he gave in.

Once, he decided.

Just this once he would allow himself to go there—to think about Kate and imagine himself with her. Or rather, Aleksi corrected as his hand slid around his heated length, just one last time.

Just one time more.

CHAPTER TWO

'You look pretty!' Georgie said as Kate sliced off the top of her boiled egg.

'Thank you,' Kate replied with a half-smile. After all, Georgie was her number one fan, and it was a compliment that was regularly given.

'Really pretty.' Georgie frowned. 'You're wearing lots of lipstick.'

'Am I?' Kate said vaguely.

'Is that new?' Her knowing little eyes roamed over Kate's new suit.

'I've had it for ages.' Kate shrugged, adding two sweeteners to her cup of tea and wishing, wishing, *wishing* she'd kept to her diet. She'd consoled herself that it would be another two months at least before he came back, and now, thanks to the lousy Nina, Aleksi would be back in the office *today!*

'Is Aleksi coming back today?' Her daughter's shrewd eyes narrowed.

'I'm not sure...' Kate was at a loss as to what to say, stunned at the mini-witch she had created. She half expected her to wrinkle up her nose and cast a spell—but then Georgie liked Aleksi.

No, Georgie *adored* Aleksi.

Kate had thought that day at the hospital would be the

last time she would see him—had almost managed to put him to the far recesses of her mind, where he would have stayed had the occasional card not arrived from him.

The occasional hotel postcard, from far-flung places around the globe, in less than legible writing.

The odd, completely child-unfriendly toys for Georgie—like a set of Russian dolls when she was eighteen months old, and a jewellery box with a little ballerina. Oh, they'd been few and far between over the years, but, given Aleksi's communication was only slightly more erratic than Georgie's father's, they had lit up the little girl's day when occasionally they came.

Kate had struggled through part-time jobs, watching the unfolding saga of the Kolovskys in all the magazines, and when Ivan had died and Levander had renounced the Kolovsky throne the news that Aleksi was moving back to Australia had had Kate on tenterhooks—until finally, *finally,* long after his return, he had called and offered her a job she couldn't refuse.

And such was the nature of the job she had been unable to refuse, despite thorough prior negotiation that she could only work school hours, sometimes Georgie could be found in the early hours of a Sunday morning sitting by Kate's desk at work, with a takeaway breakfast in her lap, as Kate gritted her teeth and worked on the latest crisis that had erupted.

'I like Aleksi!'

'Well, you would,' Kate said drily. 'He's always nice to *you.*' Even when he was at his meanest, even when Kate had somehow managed to erase six months of figures and had tearfully been trying to retrieve them as he hovered like a black cloud over her shoulder one very early morning, still he'd managed a smile and an eye-roll for Georgie.

'Mummy will find them, Georgie,' he had assured the little girl.

'Mummy damn well can't,' Kate had growled.

'Yes, Kate,' Aleksi had said, 'you can. And,' he had added, winking to his latest fan, 'don't swear in front of your daughter.'

'Does Aleksi have a girlfriend?' Georgie probed, and Kate hesitated.

Aleksi cast new meaning on the term 'playing the field', and Georgie was way too young for that. Still, she didn't want her daughter getting too many ideas on her mother's behalf.

'Aleksi's very popular with the ladies,' Kate settled for, and then tried to hurry things along. 'Come on, eat up—you've got school.'

'I don't want to go.'

'You'll enjoy it when you're there,' Kate said assuredly. But, seeing Georgie's eyes fill up with tears, she had trouble wearing that brave smile.

'They don't like me, Mum.'

'Do you want me to have another word with Miss Nugent?'

Kate had had many words with the teacher. Georgie was gifted—incredibly clever. She could read, she could write, but she was also funny and naughty and almost five years old. And Miss Nugent had more pressing problems than a child who *could* read and write.

'Then they'll be more mean to me.' Her voice wobbled and tore straight through Kate's heart. 'Why don't they like me?'

There was no simple answer. Georgie had had a miserable year at kindergarten and now school was proving no better. Though her daughter ached to join in with the other children at playtime, the other little girls didn't include her, because in the classroom she didn't fit in. She could read and write already; she could tell the time. Bored, she annoyed the other students, and the teachers too with her incessant questions, and there had been a few *incidents* recently where Georgie—Kate's sweet, happy little Georgie—had been labeled as 'difficult'.

Shamefully, it was almost a relief to Kate that Georgie didn't want her to speak to Miss Nugent!

Bruce the dog got most of Georgie's egg and toast, and as they drove to school it took all Kate's effort to keep wearing that smile as she walked a reluctant Georgie across the playground and into her classroom.

'Come on now, Georgie!' Miss Nugent said firmly as Georgie lingered by the pegs—though at least today she didn't cry. 'Say goodbye—Mum has to go to work.'

'Bye, Mum,' Georgie duly said, and it almost broke Kate's heart.

All the little girls were in groups, chatting and laughing, whereas Georgie sat alone, looking through her reader, her pencil case in front of her. How Kate wished Georgie could just join in and play. How Kate wished her daughter could, for once, fit in.

As she drove to work, not for the first time she reconsidered Aleksi's offer—if she worked full-time for him, he had told her, then he would pay for Georgie's education. Kate had already found the most wonderful school—a school with a gifted children's programme—one that understood the problems along with the rewards of having a child that was exceptionally bright. But, more importantly, Kate had known the moment she had stepped into the class during the tour that Georgie would instantly fit in.

There, Georgie would be just a regular child.

Hitting a solid wall of traffic on the freeway, she

shook her head and turned on the radio. Georgie needed a mum more than Aleksi needed a full-time, permanently on call PA, and Aleksi's moods changed like the wind—Kate couldn't let Georgie glimpse a future that might so easily be taken away if Aleksi Kolovsky suddenly changed his mind about paying for her education.

Kate wouldn't be so beholden to him.

'It's good to see you, sir.'

Normally Aleksi would have at least nodded a greeting to the doorman, but not this morning. As his driver had opened the car door he had remembered the steps that led up to the golden revolving doors of the impressive city building that was the hub of the House of Kolovsky.

He had not yet mastered steps—but he would this morning.

It had taken an hour to knot his tie—that once effortless, simple task had been an exercise in frustration this Monday morning—but no one would have guessed from looking at him. Immaculate, he walked from the car to the entrance, negotiating the steps as if it had not been four months of hell since he'd last done it. But the ease of his movements belied the supreme effort and concentration Aleksi was inwardly exerting.

'Aleksi?' Kate heard the whisper race through the building. 'What do you mean he's here?'

She could sense the panic, the urgency, but she pretended not to notice. Instead she sat at her desk, coolly typing away, glad—so glad—for the extra layer of foundation she had put on this morning, and wondering if it would stand up to Nina's scrutiny.

Aleksi's area was always a flurry of activity. He had his own vast office, but around that was an open-plan area which he often frequented—Kate worked there, as did Lavinia, the assistant PA. Kate could feel several sets of eyes on her as Aleksi's mother approached.

'Did you know about this?' Nina demanded as she stopped beside Kate's desk.

'Know what?' Kate frowned.

'Aleksi is on his way up!' Nina hissed, her eyes narrowing. 'If I find out you had anything to do with this, you can kiss your perky little job goodbye,'

'I don't know what you're talking about.' Kate swallowed and tried to feign genuine shock at the news. 'Aleksi isn't supposed to back for months yet.'

Just his presence in the building set off a panic.

There was a stampede for the restrooms as everyone dashed to fix their face. Accountants, who had been resting on their laurels, seemingly safe in the knowledge that the astute Aleksi's return was ages away, suddenly flooded Kate's e-mail inbox and phone voicemail with demands for reports, figures, meetings.

Though outwardly unruffled, inside Kate was a bundle of nerves, her heart hammering beneath her new jacket and blouse, her lips dry beneath the glossy new lipstick, her hands shaking slightly as she tapped out a response to one of the senior buyers. Even as her head told her to stay calm, her body struggled with the knowledge that, after the longest time, in just a few seconds, finally she would see him again.

She sensed him, smelt him, tasted him almost, before she faced him.

His formidable, unmistakable presence filled the entire room and her eyes jerked up as he approached— and she remembered.

Remembered the shock value of his presence—how the energy shifted whenever he was close.

It wasn't precisely that she had forgotten. She'd merely refused to let herself remember.

'What are you doing here, Aleksi?' Kate didn't have to feign the surprise in her voice; the sight of him ensured that it came naturally. A couple of months ago there had been a single photo of him captured by a *paparazzo* that had been sold for nearly half a million dollars. It had showed a chiselled and pale Aleksi recuperating in the West Indies, his wasted leg supported on pillows, and that was the Aleksi Kate had been expecting—a paler version of his old self.

Instead he stood, toned, taut and tanned and radiating health, his rare beauty amplified.

'It's good to have you back, Aleksi,' Lavinia purred. 'You've been missed.'

He just nodded and headed to his office, calling over his shoulder for a coffee. Then, as Lavinia jumped up, he specified his order. 'Kate.'

'Poor you!' Lavinia's cooing baby voice faded as Kate made his brew. 'If Nina finds out you had anything to do with him coming back she'll make your life hell.'

'I didn't,' Kate said. 'Anyway, Aleksi's head of Kolovsky, not Nina.'

'This week.' Lavinia smirked. 'Don't you realise times are changing? Aleksi's days are numbered.'

Which was the reason Kate had summoned him back.

When the youngest male Kolovsky, the head of the empire, had spectacularly crashed his car and come close to losing his life, the population of Australia had held its breath as Aleksi had lain unconscious—although rumors of brain damage and amputation had been quickly squashed. Still, the spin doctors had had other things to deal with at the same time. The news that Levander

Kolovsky had been raised in an orphanage in Russia while his father had lived in luxury with his wife had slipped out.

The House of Kolovsky had faced its most telling time, and yet somehow it had risen above it—Nina, a tragic figure leaving the hospital after seeing Aleksi, had somehow procured sympathy. Her almost obscene fortune and the rash of scandals had been countered by her recent philanthropic work in Russia. Her daughter's wedding, followed by the news that Levander was about to adopt a Russian orphan, and now her involvement with the European magnate Zakahr Belenki, who ran outreach programmes on the streets of Russia, all boded well for Nina. Suddenly the tide of bad opinion had turned, and Kolovsky could do no wrong.

'Tell the press that the House of Kolovsky is riding high.' Nina had said at a recent decisive board meeting. 'At the moment we can do no wrong.'

'And Aleksi?' the press officer had asked. 'We should give an indication as to his health—assure the shareholders his return is imminent.'

But instead of moving to communicate Aleksi's chances of full recuperation, Nina had chosen the 'no comment' route. Sitting in on the meeting, Kate had been stunned to hear his own mother's words.

'Without Aleksi at the helm,' Nina had clarified, 'Kolovsky can do no wrong.'

Two hours later, Kate had made the call to her boss.

'It's Nina you want to keep sweet! Not Aleksi!' Lavinia broke into Kate's thoughts, and suddenly she'd had enough.

'Actually, it's you I feel sorry for, Lavinia,' Kate

shot back. 'We all know what *you* have to do to keep in with the boss—I can't imagine the taste of Nina after Aleksi!'

'You're shaking,' Aleksi noted as the coffee cup rattled to a halt on his desk.

'Don't give yourself the credit!' Kate blew her fringe skywards. More than anything she hated confrontation, yet it was all around, and she simply couldn't avoid it any longer. 'I just had words with Lavinia.'

'Not long ones, I hope,' Aleksi said. 'They'd be wasted on her.'

'Oh, they were pretty basic.'

For once, there was no witty retort from Aleksi. The walk had depleted him. His leg was throbbing, the muscles in spasm, but he did not let on. Instead he took a sip of his brew and finally—after weeks of hospital slop and maids in the West Indies attempting to get it right— finally it was. He liked his coffee strong and sweet, and was tired of explaining that that didn't mean adding just a little milk. Aleksi liked a lot of everything. He took another sip and leant back in his chair, returning her smile when she spoke next.

'The place is in panic!' Kate gave a little giggle. 'I had a frantic call from Reception to alert me you were on your way up, and then the place just exploded! I even saw Nina running for the first time.'

'Running to delete all the files she is so busy corrupting,' he said cynically.

'She wants Kolovsky to do well.' Kate frowned.

'Money is her only god.' Aleksi shrugged. 'Three more months and there would have been no more House of Kolovsky ,' he sneered. 'Or not one to be proud of.'

'Things aren't that bad,' Kate answered dutifully,

but she struggled to voice the necessary enthusiasm. On paper everything was fine—fantastic, in fact—but since Levander had returned to the UK and Nina had taken over things were fast unravelling. 'I should never have called you.'

'I'm glad that you did. I've been on the phone with Marketing—"Every woman deserves a little piece of Kolovsky!"' Aleksi scorned. 'That is my mother's latest suggestion. Apart from tampering with the bridal gowns and *Krasavitsa*, she is considering a line of bedlinen for a supermarket chain.'

'An *exclusive* chain,' Kate attempted, but Aleksi just cursed in Russian.

'Chush' sobach'ya!' He glanced down at the coffee and found she was setting out an array of pills beside it. 'I don't need them.'

'I've looked at your regime,' Kate said. 'You are to take them four-hourly.'

'That was my regime when lying on a beach—here, I need to think.'

'You can't just stop taking them,' Kate insisted. She had known this was coming. Even in hospital he had resisted every pill, had stretched the time out between them to the max, refusing sedation at night. Always he was rigid, alert—even when sleeping.

So many hours she had spent by his bed during his recovery—taking notes, keeping him abreast of what was going on, assuring him she would keep him informed but that surely he should rest. She had watched as sleep continually evaded him. Sometimes, regretfully almost, he had dozed, only to be woken by a light flicking on down the hall, or a siren in the distance.

She had hoped his time away in the Caribbean would mellow him—soften him a little, perhaps. Had hoped that the rest would do him good. Instead he was leaner and if anything meaner, more hungry for action, and, no matter how he denied it, he was savage with pain.

'Get my mother in here.'

'I'm here.' Nina came in. She was well into her fifties, but she looked not a day over forty—as if, as Aleksi had once said to Kate, she had stepped straight out of a wind tunnel. She had lost a lot of weight since Ivan's death, and was now officially tiny—though her size belied her sudden rise in stature at House of Kolovsky. Dressed in an azure silk suit, her skinny legs encased in sheer black stockings and her feet dressed up in heels, with diamonds dripping from her ears and fingers, her new-found power suited her. She swept into the room, ignoring Kate as she always did. Lavinia came in behind her.

'It is good to see you back, Aleksi,' Nina said without sentiment, and Kate could only wonder.

This was her son—her son who had been so very ill, who had clawed his way back from the most terrible accident—and this was how she greeted him.

'Really?' Aleksi raised an eyebrow. 'You don't sound very convincing.'

'I'm concerned,' Nina responded. 'As any mother would be. I think that it's way too soon.'

'It's almost too late,' Aleksi snapped back. 'I've seen your proposals.'

'I specifically said you were *not* to be worried with details!' She glared over to Kate, who stood there blushing. 'Leave us!' she ordered. 'I will deal with you later. I assume this is your doing.'

'It was *your* doing,' Aleksi corrected. '*Your* grab for cash that terminated my recuperation. You may leave,' he told Kate, and she did.

It was a relief to get out of there, to be honest.

And oh, so humiliating too. Before the door closed she heard Nina's bitchy tones. 'Tell your PA she is supposed to remove the coat hanger *before* she puts on her skirt.' Kate heard Lavinia's mirthless laugh in response to Nina's cruel comment and fled to the loos, but there was no solace there.

Mirrors lined the walls and she saw herself from every angle.

Even her well-cut grey suit couldn't hide the curves—curves that wouldn't matter a jot anywhere else, but at the House of Kolovsky broke every rule. She turned heads wherever she went, and not in a good way. And by the end of the day, no matter how she tamed it, or smothered it in serum or glossed it and straightened it, her hair was a spiral mass of frizzy curls. Her make-up, no matter how she followed advice, no matter how carefully she applied it, had slid off her face by lunchtime, and her figure—well, it simply didn't work in the fashion industry.

Kate pretended to be washing her hands as an effortless beauty came in and didn't even pretend she was here for the loo. She just touched up her make-up, hoiked her non-existent breasts a little higher in her bra and played with her hair for a moment before leaving.

She didn't acknowledge Kate—didn't glance in her direction.

Kate was nothing—no challenge, no competition. Nothing.

If only she knew, Kate thought, watching in the mirror as the trim little bottom wiggled out on legs that should surely snap.

If only *they* knew her secret.

That sometimes... Kate stared in the mirror at the glitter in her eyes, a small smile on her lips as she recalled the memories she and Aleksi occasionally made.

Sometimes, when Georgie was at her grandparents', Aleksi would come to her, would leave the glitz and the glamour and arrive on her doorstep in the still of the night.

They never discussed it. He was always gone by the morning. And it wasn't as if they slept together. In fact in their entire history they'd shared just two kisses— one when Georgie was born; one the night before the accident.

And, yes, a kiss from a Kolovsky meant very little. It was currency to them, easily earned, carelessly spent, but for Kate it was her most treasured memory.

Oh, if only they knew that sometimes, late in the night, Aleksi Kolovsky came to *her* door, wanting *her* company.

'You're to go in.' Lavinia sat scowling when Kate returned, clearly annoyed at having been asked to leave the meeting.

Stepping into the room, had she not known, Kate would never have guessed the two people in there were mother and son. The air sizzled with hatred, and the tension was palpable. Aleksi was on the telephone, speaking in Arabic—just one of his impressive skills—but when he replaced the receiver he wasted no time getting straight to the point.

'Nina has agreed to delay a formal proposal to the board for a fortnight, but she will then propose her takeover of the company, with the board to vote in two months.'

Kate couldn't look at him as he spoke, so her eyes flicked to Nina instead—not a muscle flickered in her Botoxed face.

'My mother says the board is concerned by my behaviour, and that she is worried about my health and the pressure.' He dragged out each syllable, his lips curling in distaste, but still Nina sat impassive. 'I want Kolovsky and Krasavitsa to be treated as two separate entities in the vote. In return, Nina wants the full trajectory reports for Krasavitsa, along with past figures...'

Krasavitsa meant *beautiful woman*, and was a clothing and accessories range aimed at the younger market. The garments and jewels were still extravagant and expensive, still eagerly sought, but not, as was Kolovsky, exclusive.

The idea and its inception had been Aleksi's. In fact it had been his first major project when he had taken over the helm. The launch had gone well. Krasavitsa was the toast of Paris—and every young, beautiful, rich girl, according to their figures, surely by now had at least one piece in their wardrobe, or in their underwear drawer.

And when that beautiful young woman matured into full womanhood, as Aleksi had said at numerous board meetings, she would crave Kolovsky.

It had been Aleksi's pet, and he had nurtured it from the very start—but, it would seem, not satisfied just with Kolovsky, Nina wanted Krasavitsa too.

'Nina has all the figures,' Kate said, and then swallowed as Nina snorted.

'The *real* figures,' Nina said. 'Not the doctored version. I want the real figures.'

'It might take a while.' Aleksi's voice was tart. 'There are other things I need to sort out before I go through figures. The call I just took was from Sheikh Amallah's private secretary...'

Kate watched as only then did Nina show a hint of nervousness, her tongue bobbing out to moisten her lower lip.

'It would take thousands of the cheap, rubbish wedding dresses you have in mind to match the price of his daughter's Kolovsky gown.' Even though he wasn't shouting, it was clear Aleksi was livid. 'Yet you couldn't even be bothered to meet her at the airport!'

'I had Lavinia go!' Nina said defensively.

'Lavinia!' Aleksi gave a black laugh, then whistled through his teeth. 'You just don't get it, do you? You really don't understand.' He looked over to Kate. 'Arrange dinner, and then tell them Nina is looking forward to it.'

'I'm not going to dinner tonight!' Nina spoke as if he'd gone completely mad. 'You go,' she said. 'You speak their language.'

'I hardly think the Sheikh will want his virgin daughter going out for dinner with me!' Now *he* shouted. Now he *really* shouted! 'For now, *I'm* in charge, and don't forget it. For now, at least, we do things *my* way.'

'Well, I want those figures by next Monday.' Nina glowered at Aleksi. 'Only then will I make my decision.'

'You can fight me on Kolovsky,' Aleksi said. 'But I will never concede Krasavitsa. That was *my* idea.'

'Krasavitsa would be *nothing* without *my* husband's name…'

And that, Kate realised as she watched a muscle leap in Aleksi's cheek, was what appeared to hurt the most. A blistering row with his mother didn't dent him, but the insinuation that without Kolovsky he was nothing was the thing that truly galled him.

'You have *no* idea what you are doing.' Aleksi stared at his mother. 'Follow your plans and the Kolovsky name will be worth nothing in a few years.'

'These are tough times Aleksi,' Nina stood to leave. 'We have to do what it takes to survive.'

He just sat there when she had left.

'*Is* Kolovsky in trouble?' Kate couldn't help but ask.

'It will be.' Aleksi shook his head in wonder. 'We are doing well—but she strikes fear where there is none.' He rested his elbows on his desk and pressed his fingers to his temples. 'Belenki has suggested these off-the-peg bridal gowns and the bedding range. It is supposed to be a one-off—just for a year—with ten percent of the profits going to both our charities: his outreach work in Russia and the orphanages my mother sponsors.' He looked up to her. 'What do you think, Kate?'

He'd never asked her opinion on work before, but before she could reply he did so for her.

'It sounds like a good idea,' he said, and reluctantly she nodded. 'But I know it will be the beginning of the end for Kolovsky. Belenki surely also knows that; exclusivity is why Kolovsky has survived this long. I don't like him...' He halted, then frowned when Kate agreed.

'You said you didn't trust him.'

Aleksi's eyes shot to hers. 'When?'

'The night before the accident...' Her face was on fire. 'When you came to my home.' But clearly he was uncomfortable with the memory, because he snapped back into business mode.

'Get the figures ready for me,' Aleksi said. 'The real figures. But don't give them to Nina until I've gone through them.'

'She'll know if you change them.'

'She couldn't read STUPID if it was written in ten-foot letters on the wall,' Aleksi said. 'Just get them ready for me.' As she turned to go, he called her back. 'You're in or you're out.'

'I'm sorry?' Kate turned around.

'You're on my side, or you pack your bags and go now.'

She frowned at him. 'You know I'm on your side.'

'Good.' Aleksi said, but he didn't let it drop there. 'If you choose to stay, and I get even a hint that you're looking for work elsewhere, not only will I fire you on the spot, don't even *think* to put me down as a reference—you won't like what I say.'

'Don't threaten me, Aleksi. I do have rights!' Her blush wasn't just an angry one, it was embarrassment too, because, given the conversation they'd just had, she'd already decided her night would be spent online, firing off her résumé. But he had no idea what she was going through right now—no idea just how dire her finances were at this moment.

'Exercise your rights.' Aleksi shrugged. 'Just know I don't play nice.'

'I don't get your skewed logic, Aleksi.' Kate was more than angry now. 'All you had to do was *ask* that I stay, but instead you go straight for the jugular each time!'

'I find it more effective.' He looked over to where she stood. 'So you weren't considering leaving?'

'Not really.' Kate swallowed. 'But if Nina does win...' She closed her eyes. 'Not that she will—but if she does...' Hell, maybe she wouldn't get an award for dogged devotion to her boss, but it came down to one simple fact. 'I've got a daughter to support.'

'Then back a winner.' Aleksi said. 'Are you in or out?'

God, he gave her no room, no space to think. But that was Aleksi—he hurled his orders and demanded rapid response.

'I'm in.'

'Good,' Aleksi responded. 'But if I find out—'

'Aleksi,' Kate broke in, 'I've said that I'm in, that I'm not going to look for anything else. You're just going to have to trust me.'

His black smile didn't even turn the edges of his mouth. 'Why would I?'

She just loathed him at times.

Back at her desk, she loathed him so much she was tempted to have a little surf and find a job—just to prove him right!

Just to prove her word wasn't enough.

Just to convince him that his eternally suspicious mind was again merited.

And then he walked past, his leg dragging just slightly, and she watched as Lavinia gave him an intimate smile and tried to engage him in conversation that would be fed back to Nina.

His own mother was trying to destroy him.

Why would he trust anyone?

Why would he even contemplate trusting her?

All Kate knew was that he could.

CHAPTER THREE

RIMINIC IVAN KOLOVSKY.

Aleksi put the name into an internet search engine and got nothing.

He didn't really know where to start, and then he glanced over to his mother, who was going through the messages on her phone, and toyed with flicking the name on an e-mail to her, just to watch her reaction—except Lavinia was buzzing like an annoying fly around him, asking for a password so she could get some figures that were needed for tonight.

'Kate will sort it out,' Aleksi uttered, without looking over from the computer, saying the same words he spoke perhaps a hundred times a day.

It was Friday afternoon, but there was no end-of-week buoyancy filling the building. Aleksi had been back for a week now, and had made it exceptionally clear that, whatever Nina or the board might think, for now he was certainly in charge.

There had been several sackings—anyone who had dared question him had been none too politely shown the door—and everyone was walking on eggshells around him.

Everyone, that was, but Kate. She had long since

learnt that Aleksi smelt fear like a shark smelt blood, and she refused to bend to his will.

Refused to be beholden to him.

It was the only way she knew how to survive.

'I really need to get things prepared for your conference call with Belenki,' Lavinia insisted. 'The meeting won't be till six p.m. our time, and Kate leaves at five...'

There was more than a slight edge to her voice, and Kate looked up, saw the dart of worry in Lavinia's eyes, and knew for certain then that Lavinia was gathering information for Nina.

'She *has* to pick up Georgie.'

'Actually, I don't tonight,' Kate said sweetly. 'So there's no problem, Lavinia. I'll sort out the meeting.'

Aleksi chose not to notice the toxic current, but carried on with his work. He didn't look over, and neither did Kate look up as Lavinia huffed out.

'You look tired,' he commented.

Which dashed the forty minutes that she'd spent that morning in front of the mirror!

'I haven't been getting much sleep.'

'Look...' Aleksi was a smudge uncomfortable. 'What I said on Monday—'

'Has nothing to do with it,' Kate interrupted. 'I've been up at night with Georgie.'

'How is she?' Aleksi asked.

'She's just having a few problems settling in at school.' Kate tried to sound matter-of-fact. 'But she's doing well.'

'Still too well?' Aleksi asked, and Kate managed a smile at the fact that he had remembered her plight from before the accident. 'You were going to speak with the school?'

'I did,' Kate said. 'They've tried to be accommodating. They're going to see how she goes and then assess her. They might put her up a year...'

'She's not even five yet.'

'But she's so bright.'

'She should still be mixing with five-year-olds— laughing and playing with them—not sitting with the six and seven-year-olds who think she's a baby and whose work she can already do!'

Aleksi got it.

He was the one person who truly got it.

'Did you look at the school I suggested?'

'Yes,' Kate said. 'But I wish I hadn't.'

'The offer is still there. You can work full-time—I have told you that I will fund Georgie's education if you are able to make more of a commitment.' He must have read her worried frown. 'With or without the House of Kolovsky, Kate, I'll more than survive. I'll always need a full-time PA.'

'The size of the commitment you require, Aleksi, is one I can only give my daughter.' She hated him sometimes—hated the carrot he dangled in front of her because she so badly wanted it. She *wanted* that education for Georgie, but what she didn't want was a nanny for when Kate inevitably had to traipse around the world following Aleksi, when she worked till midnight, or had to leave mid-race at the school athletics carnival because some VIP had arrived and couldn't negotiate the walk from Arrivals to the awaiting limo without her...

Aleksi Kolovsky's full-time PA could not be the mother she wanted to be to her little girl.

'She'll be fine where she is,' Kate said, without any hope of believing herself.

'Please!' Aleksi snorted. 'She'll be cleverer than her

teachers soon!' He said it with a conviction that came from experience. 'Bored and restless and getting into trouble.'

'I'm saving for a good secondary school.'

She would be. Aleksi knew that. He admired her for it, and for her decision not to work full-time for him too—but it also annoyed him. He wanted her full time, wanted her quiet efficiency. It galled him that the one PA he could work with refused to commit to him.

Aleksi always, *always* got what he wanted. 'She needs her peers. She needs children her own age to play with.'

'*You* didn't have that,' Kate said, because Aleksi had been home-schooled. 'And you seem to have done all right. Iosef too!'

'I hated every moment.' He looked over to her. 'By the time I was fourteen there was nothing my tutor could teach me. By the time I was sixteen... Well, at that point there was a little more. While Iosef studied to be a doctor, I worked with my teacher one-to-one on... we'll call it lessons in human biology...'

Her cheeks were flaming. Sometimes she didn't know if he said things to get a reaction from her—to shock her, to embarrass her.

'She was a very good teacher!' Aleksi said, and then smirked. 'But, again, by seventeen already I knew more than her. At seventeen and a half I was showing her how things could better be done...'

Cheeks still flaming, Kate stood up. Aleksi laughed. 'Have I embarrassed you, Kate?'

'Not at all,' Kate said coolly, 'I'd love to stay and reminisce about your depraved childhood, but I've got the Princess arriving and I need to escort her to her fitting and make sure everything is in order.'

'Given she's already met her, surely Lavinia can do it?'

'But I'll do it better,' Kate said firmly.

'Really?'

And then their eyes locked and her blush wouldn't fade and her lungs were hot with breath that tasted of fire and she felt as if they'd just crossed a line.

It hadn't been anything other than a point she often made—Lavinia *was* rubbish with the dignitaries. She didn't get the nuances, especially with Arabian visitors. It would be far, far easier for Kate to greet their esteemed guests—see the father to the elevator and then walk with the mother of the bride and the Princess herself to the hallowed fitting rooms, which only the most pampered bride ever glimpsed.

A Kolovsky bridal gown was worth a fortune, and not a small one either.

The PAs of the newly rich and famous often had to put up with tantrums and tears when their spoiled brides-to-be finally understood that the price of a personally designed and fitted Kolovsky gown worked out to cost more than their luxurious wedding and honeymoon combined.

Both Ivan and Levander had refused to include a bridal range in Kolovsky's ready-to-wear lines. Even Aleksi, with the opening of Krasavitsa, would not put bridalwear in it.

If the bride wore Kolovsky she was someone—but not if Nina had her way.

Only they weren't talking about bridal gowns now.

'I'm quite sure,' Aleksi said, his dark eyes searing into hers, 'that you'd be wonderful.'

It was Kate who looked away first.

Never had they flirted.

Not once at work had there been an exchange.

She blushed often—but only at his debauchery.

Not once had there been...

She couldn't even really work out what had happened as she walked away from him to greet the bride-to-be. And she might just as well have sent Lavinia, because with her mind still on Aleksi it was almost impossible to concentrate on the Princess as Security opened up and they walked into the bridal area.

It was a jewel of a place that few witnessed.

Every House of Kolovsky boutique was a work of art in itself—but this was not a boutique; this was Kolovsky Bridal and it was hallowed ground indeed.

There were no walls or ceiling as such. As they walked towards the centre there were simply endless stretches of the most divine silks—the palest of blush-pinks, and every shade of cream—handmade silk that the skin ached to feel. It was like being pulled into a silken womb with each step. The huge antique mirrors were not just for aesthetics. Already the team were watching the soon-to-be bride—her posture, her figure, her gait—their brilliant minds already working on the ultimate creation for this woman, whose beauty, hidden or otherwise, was as of this moment the only thing on their minds.

There was no second store, no chain, no Kolovsky designers jetting overseas to take measurements.

Kolovsky did not chase anyone—to wear their art, you had to be present.

Of course their client would stay in Melbourne for a few days—being pampered, going through designs, being measured, seeing portrayed images of the creation on the screen—and finally there would be a follow-up visit to the bride. Then, only then, did Kolovsky come to them.

A team was dispatched a week prior to the date with the creation to wherever the wedding was to be—not just style consultants for the dress, but hair and make-up artists, an entire team to ensure that the bride who wore Kolovsky was the most beautiful.

'This…' The Princess spoke only broken English as they passed lavish display cabinets which held tiaras and shoes and jewels. Those weren't what she noticed, however. The Princess did what every woman who entered this chamber did. She walked or rather was hypnotically drawn to the divine dress in the centre. 'This one. I choose this one.'

'This is not to be reproduced,' Kate explained. 'This is the Kolovsky dress, designed for a Kolovsky or a soon-to-be Kolovsky bride.'

'I want,' the princess said, and her mother nodded—because there was nothing on God's earth that this family could not afford…except what was not for sale.

'Your dress will be designed with only you in mind,' Kate explained. 'This dress was designed for someone else.'

The design team took over then, coming out to greet the bride and her mother, pulling her into the very centre, and as the Princess went Kate watched as she gave one last lingering look at the gown on display.

There could never be anything more beautiful.

Georgie never wrapped herself in sheets or put a towel on her head as a make-believe veil—but Kate had done. She had adored dressing up as a child and, watching a royal wedding on the television, had wanted, wished, *hoped* that one day she would be as beautiful as the bride who walked blushing up the aisle towards her prince. Her mother had said that she had a good imagination—which she had—but even if her imagination could somehow transform her from tubby and serious to petite and pleasing, her secret, wildest dreams could never have conjured up this dress...

Kolovsky silk, so rumour had it, was like an opal—it changed with the mood of the woman whose skin it clung to. Each time Kate saw the dress it seemed slightly different—golden, silver, white, even transparent. Sewn into the bodice were tiny jewels, and there were more hidden in the hem, just as Ivan and Nina had hidden their treasures when they fled Russia for the haven of Australia.

This dress should have been passed, like a revered christening gown, down through the brothers' brides and then to Annika, Ivan and Nina's daughter.

But instead in turn each had shunned it.

Millie, Levander's wife, had come the closest to being married in it, but on her wedding day she had taken off the gown, left it like a puddle on the floor, and fled—only to marry Levander hours later in a jeans-clad ceremony.

Second son Iosef's wedding had taken place in the weeks after Ivan's death, and he and his wife, Annie, had felt it improper to have a lavish celebration while everyone was grieving, so the bride had worn off-the-peg lilac.

His sister Annika's wedding had taken place at Aleksi's bedside, after the accident.

Only Aleksi remained—so presumably the dress would stay where it was: locked behind glass.

'Daydreaming?' Aleksi made her jump as he walked up behind her.

'No,' Kate lied. 'What are you doing down here?'

'Just making sure everything's in place for our esteemed guest.'

'It's all going smoothly—she's in with the design team. They're looking forward to dining with Nina again tonight. Oh, and I rang your sister. Annika's agreed to go along too this time—I thought it better that we make an extra effort, given that we might have offended.'

'You've got more of an idea than Nina. Imagine her at the helm! We'll have name badges and cash registers…'

'And charge extra for a carrier bag!' Kate joined in the joke and then stared back to the dress, a question on the tip of her tongue. But she swallowed it.

'What,' Aleksi demanded, 'is your question?'

'Is there any point asking?'

'Probably not,' he said, and then relented. 'Try.'

'Why did Millie run away from her wedding?'

'You know I'm not going to answer that.' He saw her eyes narrow. 'The House of Kolovsky is a house of secrets.'

'And of course *your* secrets are far better than anyone else's.' She was annoyed.

The past weeks had been hell—toying with whether or not to ring Aleksi, risking her job by doing so, because if Aleksi had been unable to return and her indiscretion had been outed Nina would have dismissed her in a heartbeat. And yet Aleksi strolled in, asked her about her daughter, about her problems, her life, and gave her nothing of his.

'You're a snob, Aleksi, even with your family shame.'

'But our secrets *are* so much better than yours,' Aleksi teased, as he often did. Except this time, instead of enjoying the banter as she always had in the past, Kate promptly burst into tears. He was a mite taken aback. He had never seen her cry, not once—not even the day he had visited her in the hospital, where she'd lain alone after a long, arduous birth…

'What is it?' he demanded.

'What do you think?' She was suddenly angry. 'What the hell do you *think* is wrong?'

'Oh!' Aleksi suddenly looked uncomfortable. 'I'm sorry. I forget these things…'

'I don't believe you!' She didn't. 'You think I've got PMT?' Her mouth was agape, because that was *so* Aleksi! 'How about I'm suffering from YND!'

'YND?' Aleksi frowned.

'You Nearly Died!' It tumbled out of her—and he just didn't get it. Didn't get how hellish this past week had been, these past *months*, Kate clarified to herself, and realised she had never fathomed all that she was holding in. There was Georgie, up at night with bad dreams, Nina being poisonous at work, money problems, Aleksi hurt and on top of all that—or rather buried beneath all that—the hell of his accident, the sheer fright that had come, which had still not been processed, when she had been informed by Iosef that Aleksi had had an accident and might not make it through the night.

There was a fabulous coffee area on the second floor but she couldn't face that, so they headed out of the golden doors and across the street, and she sat in a coffee shop as he fed her napkins and she snivelled into them.

'I thought you were going to die!' Kate wailed. 'We were told you *could* well die.'

'But I didn't,' came his logical reply.

'And now here you are—back, as if nothing has happened…'

'Kate.' Aleksi shook his head, moved to correct her, then halted himself. He certainly wasn't going to reveal to her, or to anyone, just how much *had* changed. How he struggled with so many things that sometimes he wondered if he *should* be back at work. Because he was running a massive empire, yet without thinking really hard he couldn't even remember how many sugars he had in his own coffee. 'I'm fine…'

'I know you are!' She was being unreasonable, illogical. She wished she had fled to the loos to weep, instead of sitting in this public place with him. 'It was just…'

'Just what?'

'Seeing you like that,' she settled for. 'You were still so badly hurt when you went to rehab, and now…' She struggled to describe just how confusing it all was. 'Now you're back. As if nothing happened. All this stuff with your mother, Krasavitsa, the arguments, Belenki…' She screwed her eyes closed, took a deep breath, and tried to articulate what she was thinking. 'Everyone's straight back to business, but I'm just taking a little while longer than everyone else to forget just how bad things were. You nearly *died*!'

There had been no downtime, Aleksi acknowledged. No reflection, really.

Yes, he had lain in that hospital bed, but his brain had been too messed with trauma for contemplation, and in the Caribbean his mind had been too blurred with painkillers to allow anything other than for him to aim at one fixed goal: to get well, to return, to be as good as—no, better than—before.

But now, sitting in a café, perhaps for the first time he saw what he had almost lost—saw too the emotion that had been so lacking in his recovery, in his life.

'Thank you.' So rarely he said it, it felt strange to his lips. 'For all your kind thoughts and help. I hadn't realised how hard all this was on you. But I'm back now and I'm well.'

She nodded—felt a bit stupid, in fact.

'Now...' Aleksi stood. 'I have to show the world just how well I am.'

'Meaning?'

'The old Aleksi is back.'

'Shouldn't you...?'

He was about to stand to go, but when she frowned, Aleksi remained seated.

'Shouldn't I what?'

'Calm things down, perhaps?' It was far from her place to tell him how to live his life, but given the circumstances Kate took the plunge. 'Just till the board make their decision.'

'I think it might take a bit more than a few early nights to convince them I've changed. No.' Now he stood up. 'I'm not going to change just to appease them.'

'Will you think about it?'

'I just did,' Aleksi said, and gave her *that* smile that always made her stomach curl.

Although she returned it, her heart sank as they headed back and up to his office, because the moment they stepped back into the building all tenderness was gone and he was back to his usual cold, businesslike self—though he did remember to check if she was okay to stay when the clock nudged past five.

'It's no problem,' Kate said. 'My sister's picking her up from after-school care.'

'She lives in the country?'

Kate nodded, her throat just a touch dry, a dull blush spreading on her cheeks, but she hid it well, busying herself on the computer and trying, desperately trying, to keep her voice light. 'Yes, Georgie's staying there this weekend.'

He made no comment. She wasn't even sure if he'd heard her—didn't even know if he'd factored it in.

Kate had.

Going over and over and over the nights he'd come to her place, the only common denominator was that Georgie hadn't been home.

Had she been, Kate might not have let him in.

So she had the figures ready for the meeting with Belenki, and afterwards, when he came out with a face like thunder, she informed him she had arranged the best table at the casino for him and his date to dine that night. Then finally, after a very long day, she picked up her bag as Aleksi left for his very public night out.

He was dressed in a dinner suit.

Freshly washed, his hair was slicked back, gorgeous yet slightly unkempt, and Kate frowned.

'Did you keep your appointment?'

'Sorry?'

She glanced down at his hands, at nails that were spotless but just not as polished as usual. Every other Friday without fail Aleksi headed over to the trendiest of trendy salons, sat and drank green tea as his thick black hair was washed and trimmed, his nails buffed, his designer stubble made just a little bit more so. She had rung them during the week to say the appointments would now resume, and had told Aleksi the same.

Except his five o'clock shadow was a natural one and his hair was still just a touch too long.

'The salon—' Kate started, but Aleksi just screwed up his nose.

'Tell them they are to come to me now—I'm tired of going there.'

'Sure.' She made a quick note in her diary and said goodnight—it wasn't an unusual request. Aleksi often changed his mind, and it was her job to sort it out when he did. 'Have a good night, then,' she said to him.

'You too,' Aleksi said. 'Any plans?'

'A bath and then bed,' Kate admitted, and then she smiled. 'Or I might just hit the clubs!'

'Oh, that's right,' Aleksi said. 'You don't have Georgie tonight.'

'No.' She was standing by the lifts, and had to turn her face to concentrate on the lift buttons rather than let him see her blush. 'I'll see you on Monday.'

'Sure.'

She would, Aleksi told himself.

She would see him on Monday, and not a moment before.

He watched her leave, watched her yawn as she pressed the lift button and could, for a dangerous moment, imagine her slipping out of those shoes, peeling off that suit, sinking into a bath, relishing the end of the week, the end of the day.

For Aleksi the night had just started.

He was tired, but he blocked that thought.

He was in pain, but he refused to take another pill. It had been twenty-four hours without them and it was getting harder by the minute, but he would not take another—they messed with his head.

He headed for the lift and stared for a full three seconds. He didn't want Ground he wanted Reception. He had made the same mistake so many times this week.

Not that anyone could have guessed.

Not even Kate.

He raked back his hair with his hands, and as he stepped into the lift he closed his eyes and tried and tried again in vain to picture the location of the hair salon. His eyes snapped open as the lift doors did the same.

'Goodnight, Mr Kolovsky.'

He nodded to the receptionist. Actually responded to the doorman tonight. Made the steps with apparent ease and then slid into the back of his waiting car.

Tonight he would prove to the world he was back.

Put paid to all the rumours.

He kissed his date thoroughly. They'd been out a few times before the accident and she was delighted, she said, pressing herself into him as they sped to the casino, that he was back.

'It's good to be back,' Aleksi said, and then he kissed her again—but only because it was easier than talking. It was far easier to kiss her than to tell her that he couldn't remember her name.

CHAPTER FOUR

THERE was no thrill.

Aleksi put a million on black and just stared as the wheel went round.

Win, lose.

There was just no thrill any more.

He didn't need the money, and he didn't need Kolovsky.

Wasn't sure if he wanted either.

He won.

He could hear the cheers, turned to what was surely the most beautiful woman on this planet and accepted the kiss on his lips, but he still couldn't remember her name. He kissed her back, could taste her champagne on his sober tongue, and for a moment he pulled her in, wanted her smell, her breasts, her body to do something to cure the numbness.

Yet he couldn't even accept the toast that was raised to him, let alone raise one himself.

He was back!

His suite awaited.

Paradise awaited.

Oblivion, even.

He was fifty million richer and he couldn't even become aroused by the beautiful woman he held in his arms.

Ah, but he knew his body. Like his Midas touch, it had never once failed him—and it didn't now.

There it was—that primal response, the Kolovsky legend that never dimmed—and there was her triumphant smile as she finally felt his surge of arousal...

What *was* her name?

'Excuse me one moment.'

He had been born in Australia but schooled at home, surrounded by his family, his history, and despite his perfectionism still there was just a hint of Russian to his voice.

He walked to the restroom.

The door was held open.

He relieved himself, zipped himself back into his exquisite suit pants and then washed his hands. Then, because it was numb and it felt like plastic, he washed his face as well. He pressed it into a fluffy towel and caught his reflection in the mirror.

Black hair, thick and glossy—check.

Slate-grey eyes, not a hint of blood in their whites—check.

Smooth, unblemished skin—check.

Designer stubble—check.

The chief of Kolovsky.

He loosened his tie, because he could feel his pulse leaping against his collar.

He knew.

What it was, he couldn't remember—but he knew something important!

More than his brother Levander, who had lived it.

More than his twin, Iosef, who had *dealt* with it.

More than his sister Annika, who had worked through it.

He was cleverer than the lot of them—and being clever was a curse.

He *knew*. He knew so much more than any of them, and though he denied it—though his father had beaten him into silence because the truth would change everything—it was harder and harder to hide from it now.

There was a memory—an image, just a breath, just a realization away—yet no matter how he reached out to it, over and over it slipped from his grasp.

Why couldn't he remember?

He pressed his face into the cool mirror, willed clarity to come, and stared into the murky depths of his mind, hoping to God that coming off the pain medication would help clear it somehow. Because Aleksi knew that something had to be done.

He just didn't know what.

His phone was bleeping in his pocket, summoning him back to his immaculate world. He took a breath and headed out there, and then it bleeped again and he looked at the screen.

Brandy.

Yes, that was her name. The word was suddenly there in front of him as she called him, no doubt wondering where he was, and now he remembered her name and also a ridiculous rhyme.

Whisky makes you frisky; brandy makes you randy.

Well, not tonight.

He turned left instead of right, ended up in the kitchen instead of the high rollers' bar, ignored the exasperated attempts to turn him around, and then, when his phone beeped again, instead of answering it he rang his personal driver and told him to ensure that Brandy was taken home or put up in the hotel—whatever it was she required.

'Any message?' his driver asked.

'None,' Aleksi said, and then clicked off his phone, tossed it into a deep fat fryer and pushed open a door.

He walked down the fire escape stairs, past the skips and dumpsters, out to a side street and into a cab.

'Where to?' the driver wanted to know.

Aleksi didn't answer at first

'Where to?' the cab driver asked again.

'The airport,' Aleksi said, and as they made their way along the freeway it was all so familiar. He had been here before—he remembered then, the night of the accident, driving as if the devil was chasing him towards the airport, only he couldn't remember why. Maybe it was because it would have given him time to think, Aleksi decided. Maybe that was what he had craved that night—what he craved right now. Except the freeway was clear, the streetlights shortening, and they were there in less than thirty minutes. 'Take me back to the city.'

The cab driver started to argue, but stopped as a wad of notes silenced his protest.

'Just drive.'

So they did.

One a.m. Two a.m. They drove around.

'Left,' Aleksi said as once again the city lights receded. 'Take the exit here,' he commanded as they swerved into suburbia. 'Right at the roundabout. And right again.'

Then he saw Kate's house, nondescript in the darkness. The little streak of grass needed a cut, her car needed a wash, and a 'For Sale' sign was posted outside.

'Stop here.'

Money talked, so the taxi driver didn't—just stopped there, for five, ten, fifteen minutes, as Aleksi waited for normal services to resume, for this madness to abate, to tap the driver on the shoulder and tell him to take him back.

He had said never again.

He had sworn to himself he'd never come here again.

Hated himself for leading her on—because nothing could ever come of it.

Three times he had ended up here—and loathed himself for it.

Tomorrow, when the sun rose, he would surely regret it again.

Don't make the same mistake again, he begged himself.

But...

'Go.' He stepped out of the cab.

'I can wait,' the driver offered. 'Make sure someone's home...'

'Go,' Aleksi repeated.

He stood there, in the middle of suburbia at three a.m., with no phone, watching the cab drive off and wondering to himself what the hell he was doing here.

Again.

He quashed that thought, tried to dismiss memories of his other late night visits to this house, but they rose to the surface again, demanding an answer he struggled to give.

He'd known her the longest.

It was the first time he'd considered it, thought about it, pondered it.

Apart from family, Kate had been in his life the longest of any woman—their fractured five-year history was the furthest back he'd ever gone. Aleksi travelled light; when a relationship was over it was over, and as for female friends—well, he'd never quite worked out how to keep it at that...

But he'd had to with Kate.

He walked up the path. Stared at the door. Told himself he could handle it.

And then took a breath and knocked.

Hearing the knocking on the door, Bruce barking just a couple of moments too late to earn the title of guard dog, Kate turned on the light. Half awake and half asleep, even as she headed down the hall she told herself not to hope.

Kate sometimes wondered if she imagined these visits.

There was never any mention of them—and certainly no acknowledgment of them—afterwards.

She didn't really understand why he came, yet three times before now he had arrived on her doorstep.

Once, a couple of weeks after she had started back at Kolovsky, he had said that the press had been chasing him and he had shaken them off and ended up here. She had loaned him her sofa. His silver car had looked ridiculous in her drive and he had been gone by the time she had awoken the next morning.

Then, a few weeks later, there had been a row and she had resigned when he'd demanded she stay at work late. He had arrived in a taxi, a little the worse for wear, and had asked her to reconsider handing in her notice—had offered to more rigorously uphold the part-time conditions he had previously agreed to and then, when she had agreed to return, promptly fallen asleep on her sofa.

He had returned a third time after the charity ball, incoherent, clearly the worse for wear and at odds with everyone—furious with Belenki, with his family, and with the world. They had shared their second kiss—a sweet, confusing kiss, because even as it had ended she'd seen the conflict in his eyes. What had taken place would not be open to discussion, and again he had been gone by morning. Then the accident had happened.

But now he was back—not just at work, but in her home, too.

Cruel, restless, angry—and never more so than now—again he was at her door.

'My leg...'

She could see the sweat beading on his forehead as he limped over the threshold—which told her of the pain he was in, because this week he had hidden his limp so well. 'Have you had a pill?' She had never seen him like this. Not since the early days at the hospital, when they had been trying to get his pain medication under control. 'Maybe you need an injection?'

'I've stopped taking anything!' he gasped.

He was so pale beneath his tan she thought he might pass out.

'You're supposed to be on a reducing dose.'

'I have reduced—I've stopped completely.'

'When?'

'Today.'

'Aleksi!' She was truly horrified. 'They said you had to reduce slowly—that it would be months before you could manage without them. You can't just stop like that.'

'Well, I just did.' Aleksi said. 'I need to think straight.'

'You can't think straight if you're in pain!' Kate insisted.

'Listen!' His hand closed around her wrist, his voice urgent. 'Listen to me. Since the accident I have not been able to think straight...'

'That's to be expected.'

'Exactly.' His eyes were grey, the whites bloodshot, and she had never seen him look more ill. 'They do not want me to think straight. Since that new doctor, always there are more pills...'

'He's the best,' Kate insisted. 'Your mother researched...' Her voice trailed off—surely Nina wouldn't stoop that low? But from the way she was acting now, maybe she could.

'I am going back under the care of the hospital. I have an appointment on Monday. Once I can think, once I am off this medication, I will get them to manage things—not a doctor of my mother's choosing.' He looked over to her, and she could see pain there that was so much more than physical. 'You must think I'm being completely paranoid...'

She was silent for the longest time before she spoke. 'Regretfully, no.' She thought a moment longer. 'I think maybe we're *both* being paranoid but, yes, I can see you don't trust her.'

'If I can get through tonight then I can think straight...'

That much she understood.

There was still so much she didn't.

It should have been uncomfortable—awkward, perhaps, but when he was here in her home. It wasn't.

Oh he was scathing and loathsome and everything Aleksi, yet he travelled lighter here—even if he was in pain, it was as if all his baggage had been checked and left at the door.

'How,' he said, standing at the bathroom door, 'can you lose a plug?'

She'd suggested a bath and, given he'd probably never

run one in his life, for tonight she'd made allowances
and offered to run it for him. Except she couldn't find
the plug!

'Maybe Georgie...' Kate started. But, no, she'd had
a bath herself tonight.

'Retrace your footsteps!' was his most unhelpful suggestion.

'What about a shower?'

'You've just talked me into a bath, Kate,' Aleksi said.
'You spent the last ten minutes telling me how it would
relax me, how—'

'Here!' The plug was in one of its regular hiding
places—between the pages of a book she'd been reading—and of course he didn't let her get away with it that
easily. As she put in the plug and turned on the taps,
having checked for towels and the like, she tried to beat
a hasty retreat. But Aleksi blocked the door, holding
out his hand and taking the novel from her reluctant
hands.

'I might like to read in the bath too,' he told her.

He must, because he was gone for an age.

She didn't really know what he was doing here—what
it was that made him come. She just knew that he did.

Knew, somehow, that to question him would close the
tiny door that occasionally opened between them.

The suave, sophisticated thing to do would be not to
answer the door.

To pretend perhaps that she was out.

But she was in.

Definitely in to Aleksi.

She had a life.

A career.

A family.

But he was her thrill.

A guilty, delicious secret. An endless question that delivered no answers. But how nice he was to ponder. Unattainable to her, but for a while, at least, here with her in her home.

Oh, she knew what Aleksi was going through tonight—going cold turkey from his medication—and tomorrow, when she awoke to him gone, it would once again be Kate battling withdrawal symptoms from the loss of Aleksi.

'Does she go back to him?' He stood, leaning in her doorway, dripping wet, a towel around his hips, and Kate jumped where she lay on the bed and tried to scramble her thoughts into order. 'Jessica?'

He really had been reading it! 'For a little while,' Kate said as he walked over. Really, there was no question of the sofa for either of them; somehow she knew that tonight they were both staying here in her bedroom. 'Then…'

'Then what?' Aleksi asked, sitting on the bed. 'Then she realised she was better off without him?' He lay down beside her, stretched out, just a towel covering his loins, and she couldn't look—how she wanted to look, but she couldn't.

'I haven't got that far yet.' He closed his eyes and now she *could* look at him. Sitting up against the pillows, she stared at the most beautiful specimen of a man, lying beside her, one of her small towels a sash around his groin, his cheekbones—oh, God, his perfect cheekbones—two dark slashes on his cheeks, and the spike of wet eyelashes closed. But it was his nearly naked body that was new to her tonight—many nights of imaginings hadn't sufficed. Up close and personal, he was nothing but stunning.

'You're selling your home?' Somehow he managed to talk normally, and Kate tried for the same.

'My landlord is selling.'

Eyes still closed, he frowned, because of course he didn't really understand what it meant to her.

'That's why I asked my sister to have Georgie—I need to find somewhere this weekend.' She watched the edge of his eyes scrunch to deepen his frown.

'Surely he must give you notice?'

'I got given a month's notice,' Kate said. 'Last weekend you informed me you were flying home. This weekend I start looking. Next weekend I hope I find somewhere...' She stopped herself before her voice cracked. Kate never took the woe-is-me route, and suddenly she didn't need to to stop herself from getting upset, because then she got a little bit angry and it crept into her voice. 'That's if my employer will give me a reference.'

He opened his eyes to her.

'I came on too strong, perhaps?'

'There's no perhaps about it,' she retorted indignantly.

'I can't afford for you to leave just now.'

'That's all you had to say.'

When she looked back on this night—and it was certain that over and over she would—Kate wondered if she'd remember how she came to be touching him. But now, living it, feeling it, when it actually came to it, it was so seamless, so natural, that after a while of talking, after another while of silence and then talking again, when his leg was racked with painful cramping, it was more a response than a thought that led her hand to his thigh. Once it was there, once that jump had been made, she didn't want to return to a world without the feel of him beneath her fingers, even if she knew that tomorrow she would.

His skin was warm, firm and taut beneath her fingers, the contact firing her nerves into a frenzied alert. She wrestled to calm them, had to concentrate on slowing her breathing down as she slid her hand over the tight muscle, and then slowly the sirens in her body hushed a little, grew deliciously accustomed to the feel of him, and Kate could breathe more normally as she worked his spasmed flesh. She could see the scars where the pins and bolts had been. She took some baby oil—it was all she could think of—and squirted it on, rubbing the tense mound of flesh, tentatively at first and then more firmly. It took ages, and she wasn't even sure it was helping, but the muscle finally gave beneath her fingers. Then just after it relaxed it tensed again. She heard his curse, saw him grit his teeth, and she actually knew something about how he felt.

'When I had Georgie…'

'Don't!' He both laughed and warned her at the same time. 'Don't say you know how it feels…'

'But I do.' Still her hand worked on. 'I was on my own, and the nurses kept telling me that I was doing fine, that it was all completely normal, but I was begging for something. I couldn't believe how much it hurt. I knew childbirth was supposed to hurt, but it was agony. The pain just kept coming…'

'For how long?'

'All night,' Kate said. 'And I thought I'd never get through it, but I did.'

'I don't want drugs,' Aleksi said, and Kate smiled.

'I said the same.' She pressed her fingers harder into the tight knot of his thigh muscle, heard his hiss of breath, saw his hand go to remove hers. But the muscle finally relented, the tight spasm loosened, and she worked on.

'Did you give in?' Aleksi asked.

'Absolutely.' Kate smiled. 'I screamed the place down for everything.'

And Aleksi smiled, too. 'I won't give in.'

He wouldn't—that much she knew.

'Is it agony?'

'No.' His answer surprised her. 'It's not so much the pain…more the thoughts.'

'Thoughts?' Still her hands worked on.

'It would be easier to knock myself out,' Aleksi explained. 'But I just need to get through this.'

He'd put on muscle in his leg. The last time she had seen it, it had been withered and wasted, studded with pins and bolts. Now it was tanned and lean, with fresh scars and dark hair. When his thigh muscle was pliant she worked down, as the physio had done, and unknotted the calf muscle that bore so much of the strain of his healing thigh.

'You'll get there.' She was absolutely sure of it. 'Just relax.'

'Easier said than done,' he said wryly.

'Just try,' she pleaded.

So he did.

He lay there and thought only of her hands.

Listened to the tick, tick, tick of her little alarm clock.

He had loathed this in hospital—the invasion of his body, being told to relax, not to fight—but right now he got what they had been trying to tell him, because when he did relax, when he did let go, it was as if his muscles were melting.

He had never been better looked after.

Aleksi lay back on her bed and stared at the ceiling.

He had never been more relaxed, more comfortable with another soul.

Always he performed.

At dinner, in business, in bed, in hospital—always it was Aleksi driving the conversation, the deal, the orgasm, the recovery. Whatever the goal, he was relentless in pursuing it, but tonight—this morning—he lay there and for a little while just let her...

Let his mind, let his body, let himself just be—till the spasm hit again, his leg contracting, his mind tightening with the pain of recall, memories awakening. The screech of tyres and the smell of burning rubber, his car spinning out of control because his mind had been so full of other things. And as he lay there it was so vivid he had to clench his fists to prevent his arms flying up to shield his face.

Her hands were at the back of his thigh now, working the tight hamstring, and he wanted to shout out because it was sheer hell to remember.

'Don't think of anything,' she said gently.

So he looked at her instead of looking inside his mind. Her eyes were down in concentration. His moved lower too, to her cleavage, and he focused on that for a soothing moment, willing the gown to part, to reveal just a little bit more, but desire alone couldn't do that. Then he watched her hands work, saw his flesh move with each stroke to his thigh, felt his breathing slow down, and it was almost hypnotic the effect she had on him.

He was covered now by just the small towel which had loosened. His thigh was soft, but her tender ministrations had been recognised by his body elsewhere.

'Don't worry.' Embarrassed, she turned her face away, went to stand, tried to be matter-of-fact. 'I'm sure it happens…' Well, it must—all the physiotherapists, nurses who had touched him…

'Not once.'

And so here was her guilt.

Her never again.

Because each time he came to her door the bar shifted.

First a kiss.

Then a conversation.

Each a guilty memory that she took out and examined now and then like a precious hidden treasure.

And now this.

Her hand was still on his thigh, not moving. She could have walked away at that point, except she didn't.

This was the bit she would never understand.

Because here, alone with him in her house, away from it all and only for a short while, she felt beautiful.

For the first time in her life, when those grey eyes looked into hers, she felt as if she were another person entirely.

A bold, sensual woman.

Only she wasn't.

Sex had been mired in shame for Kate. Her first attempt with Craig had resulted in Georgie, followed closely by Craig insisting that her intention had been to trap him into marriage, then cruelly berating her for putting on weight and finally, on Kate's insistence, leaving.

Craig's relief to be leaving her had been palpable; she had actually seen his tension evaporate as she'd exonerated him of any duty to their unborn child. His parents had some contact with Georgie, and on occasion he saw his daughter there. He did send birthday presents and Christmas cards, but that was the sum total of his involvement.

As she had closed the door on him, Kate had sworn *never again*.

She was a mother, and she'd be the best mother she could be, and she'd do it without a man rather than subject Georgie to her mistakes.

But now Aleksi lay in her bed, and she was more than a mother tonight. For the first time in the longest time she was a woman again.

His eyes were on her face, and she just stared back at him, her hand still on his thigh. She moved it again, stroked him again, but it was more than a healing touch and they both knew it. She could feel his thigh contract beneath her fingers, feel the waves of pain rising within him again. But she would soothe him with a different touch now.

'Kate…' His hand moved over hers as it crept up his thigh. 'You don't have to…'

'I know.' Except she was mired in want. Yes, this would change things—but they had changed already.

Yes, she knew she could never keep him—but she wanted to have had him, at least for a little while.

She had never held a man in her hand, but she did so now. She held him as if it was her right—her fingers warm from the oil as she slid them around his thick length.

'Kate…' He said it again, almost urging her to stop, because there was a strange nervousness for Aleksi. His pain, his guilt and his shame would still be there tomorrow, but for now it all melted away with the bliss of her touch. A touch that wasn't greedy or demanding, but was instead a slow, rhythmic touch that had him staying silent and instead closing his eyes.

It was an inexperienced touch that he almost wanted to correct—to place his hand over hers in order to show her how, a better how. Except, Aleksi realised as he gave in to her ministrations, it couldn't be better than this.

There was a deep pleasure in the unexpected.

A lack of expertise brought a surprise with every delicious stroke.

It was too light.

She was scared to hurt him.

Too rough.

She couldn't help herself.

Not there.

She cupped him in her hand.

Be careful. His mind said what his mouth held back from.

Only Kate didn't hold back.

She cupped him and stroked him and was just so bowled over by his beauty, so lost in this intimate place. He was more beautiful than anyone had a right to be— *this* was more wonderful than she had ever dreamt—and this was real and he was here and she grew bolder.

She stroked him more easily now, finding her rhythm, and she felt a deep pool of excitement swell within her. Now her hands were busy, her mouth craved contact with him.

Guided by want rather than logic, she lowered her lips, kissed his flat nipple, anticipating what she didn't know—for him to tell her enough? To warn her off? But she heard his ragged breath, and she kissed it as delicately and then as hungrily as she wished he would kiss her.

She felt his hand creep into her dressing gown but she brushed it off. Hungry now for herself, she kissed down his chest and down his flat stomach. She relished each caress, each lick, savoured them because she knew she would live on this for weeks.

Till the master called for her again this would be her escape, this the moment she would relive.

Her mouth was neither skilled nor practised, but it didn't confuse.

There was a pleasure in its simplicity. He lay there, staring at the ceiling, and for a moment he wanted to climb from the bed, to tell her...what?

Yet he lay there.

She kissed him—not to impress or to please, but to appease her own building need. She tasted and she licked and she felt his fingers knot in her hair as she grew bolder, taking him deeper and relishing him.

For Aleksi it was a revelation.

To just lie there, to do no more than that.

To lie and think of nothing but her lips on him. This from a man who merely tolerated massages—though he was booked in each week.

Always he lay there, willing the hour over. Gave a huge tip, said he felt marvelous. Slipped back into his suit feeling the same, just oiled.

Till now, he had felt the same with this.

Yet for the first time all he did was lie there—no rush, no feigned moans, no urgency.

He lay there.

And then his hips rose.

Except he didn't want it over so soon.

So he lay there for a moment longer and climbed into a void where all there was was this sensation, just this moment in time.

'Kate,' he gasped, and his hips rose again. He felt moisture in his eyes, which he screwed closed.

He could feel her tender ministrations and he didn't want them to stop—but finally his body was beating its blessed relief. He had never been in a place like it—a still, silent place, where there was just her tongue and her lips and her breath and an endless night that was now only a little way from dawn.

He didn't know this place that was devoid of demand, of reciprocal rights—this unfamiliar place where he opened his eyes and looked at his generous bedfellow without resentment, of one with whom he actually still wanted to share a bed.

He pulled her up beside him, liked the curves and the flesh that he tangled into, liked the scent of her hair and the weight of her breast on his chest.

The right word had often evaded him these past months, and he did the usual search, trawled through his mind's thesaurus in a brain that had gone over its download limit. The search too slow; the answer when it came was surely wrong.

Calm.

He'd never known it or felt it, but even as he disputed it, even as he tried to come up with another word, it remained in his mind as sleep finally invaded and claimed him.

CHAPTER FIVE

SHE awoke to a bed that was, apart from her, empty. She waited for the tsunami of shame to sweep in, waited for regret, for remorse to arrive. But instead Kate just lay for a quiet moment, blinking as she realised those feelings were absent.

There wasn't a minute of last night that she regretted.

Oh, she did momentarily consider a full-face tattoo to hide her blushes when she faced him on Monday, but even as she climbed out of bed still regret was absent, still she considered that last night was very possibly the most wonderful of her life.

Kate pulled on her dressing gown, splashed her face with water, and on autopilot brushed her teeth.

She had three rental properties to look at this morning, plenty to get on with today, and she would do everything in her power not to think about Aleksi till later tonight, when she could quietly sit and go over the night they had shared.

Refusing to check her phone to see if he'd texted her, she padded out to the mail box and collected the newspaper, then headed into the kitchen.

'I've been thinking...'

'Ah!' she gasped, and almost dropped the news-paper.

It hadn't even occurred to Kate that he might still be here! Always he was gone by dawn, and the dark hours prior were conveniently forgotten by Monday. Yet here he was, in the morning sun, in her kitchen, pouring scalding water into two mugs!

'Where are the coffee beans?' he asked.

'In Kenya,' Kate said, opening a jar of instant and trying not to let him see how rattled his presence made her feel. The sight of him in her dingy kitchen brought her no comfort; she didn't actually want her two worlds colliding. Last night had been fantasy, escape—it suited her that they didn't speak about it, didn't acknowledge it, that their private moments weren't analysed in the cold light of day.

But here he was.

He had on only the bottom half of his suit. Despite arduous work-outs to regain his strength he had lost weight, and the pants sat a touch lower on his hips. Usually that would have been sorted. He had an army of designers at his disposal, after all, and Aleksi Kolovsky would have utilised them.

It was the tiniest detail, yet she noticed it.

Liked it, even.

Liked the extra glimpse of toned flat stomach and the glimpse of dark hair that led to where she had kissed him last night.

No, she did *not* like her dreams invading reality like this!

Didn't like facing him in her tatty dressing gown with her morning hair, and painfully aware of her shabby kitchen, and that he was no doubt regretting coming to her door.

Again.

'I thought you'd be gone,' she commented.

Aleksi had thought he would be gone by now too.

Always he rose early, but since the accident it had been ridiculous. His eyes snapped open long before dawn and he listened to the world wake up as he lay there, racked with exhaustion but unable to rest. Except this morning. For the first time since the accident, for the first time since way before then, even, the sun had beaten him in rising.

Refreshed, even relaxed, he had left Kate sleeping, his intention to call a cab. Yet he had been reluctant to leave, reluctant to face what needed to be faced, and, attempting to locate coffee, had seen the neat stack of bills by the microwave, recalled the 'For Sale' sign outside the house and his solution had been found.

Aleksi didn't slowly form ideas, but neither did he mull. His mind was too rapid for rumination; he scanned details most legal eyes would take hours to ponder. He cut straight to the chase. 'Move in with me.'

Kate rolled her eyes.

'You have to find somewhere to live. I have a huge home you could stay in for a couple of months...' His idea stalled as the scruffiest dog he had ever seen strolled past and Kate let him out to the back yard. 'You're not saying anything.'

'Because it doesn't warrant a response,' Kate said dryly, and got on with making a much needed cup of coffee.

'You, Georgie...' he hesitated, but only for a second '...the dog...'

'Bruce.'

'I'm going to London in a few days, to meet with Belenki,' Aleksi said. 'We need to do some straight talking. So I'll be away and you and Georgie will have the place to yourself for a while—I'd hardly be there...' Still she didn't respond. 'It could help us both out.'

'Ah, now we're getting somewhere.' Kate handed him a mug. 'How, precisely, would a single mother and her entourage living in your home help you, Aleksi?'

'It would show responsibility. It would prove to the board...' He hesitated. 'I thought about what you said—maybe I do need a change of attitude to win the board over. Let them see that I am settling down, that I am serious about the business of Kolovsky.'

'Settling down?' she repeated flatly.

'We could say you were my fiancée. Just for a couple of months—just till I get the board's vote.'

'No.'

It was a definite answer, but one Aleksi refused to accept. 'The board thinks—'

'You've never cared what the board thinks before.'

'I've never needed to. They know I do a brilliant job, they know I can run the place blindfolded, but always there is greed.'

'No.' She said it again, even shot out an incredulous laugh at his ridiculous thought process.

'You would be remunerated.'

'Two months' worth of free rent in exchange for messing up my life? I don't think so!'

'Of course not.'

And then a dream came true.

Or rather the fantasy that soothed her late in the night sometimes—the times when she lay racked with worry, scared for Georgie's future. The dream where all that was waved away by some strange miracle—only this wasn't a winning lottery ticket, nor some unknown ancient relative's legacy.

No, six feet two inches of arrogant male Kolovsky looked her straight in the eye and offered her such an outlandish sum that the third no, though on the tip of her tongue, wasn't quite so speedily delivered. The synapses in her brain were firing in rapid calculation of the future she could achieve if only she had the nerve to say yes to him.

'No,' Kate said again, except it was preceded by a swallow.

'Think about it.' He drained his mug and then walked over to her, shrinking the kitchen and making her feel impossibly claustrophobic as he stood before her. He leant forward a touch, to place his mug on the bench behind her. She could smell him, smell the danger of him, and in that moment Kate knew he was deadly serious—she had worked with him long enough to know that Aleksi didn't make idle offers.

To know that Aleksi *always* got his way.

'I've given you my answer.' She would not be intimidated. She refused to look at him, and took a sip of her drink instead.

'If I don't sort out this chaos my mother is creating, if I don't halt Belenki in the next few days, then I'm walking away from the company completely,' he said.

She felt as if she were standing on a trampoline, unsteady and unsure, watching as the springs snapped away one by one. 'You'd never leave Kolovsky!'

'Oh, I'd leave it in a heartbeat,' Aleksi responded.

'It's your life.'

'It's just business,' Aleksi answered.

Another spring snapped and any minute she'd be falling. Without Aleksi there, she'd certainly be fired. Where else could she earn so much for so few hours?

'You'd get another job, of course.' Aleksi smiled.

'You're blackmailing me,' she whispered.

'Not at all.' He shook his head. 'Before I leave I'd give you a glowing reference, saying what a brilliant PA you are—you know a Kolovsky reference will open any door. How could I possibly be blackmailing you?'

Because she didn't want to be a full-time PA—didn't want to work from seven till seven and then spend half the night on the computer and the phone.

'I am offering you a future—whatever happens at Kolovsky your future can be secured.' Aleksi's voice was like silk—raw silk, though. 'Georgie's future...'

'What about Georgie?' She was angry now—angry at him offering this without true thought, angry at herself for even letting her mind dance down the delicious path he was offering. She tried to push past him, but he caught her arms. 'What would I tell her, Aleksi? *Oh, Mummy's engaged, we're moving in...*'

'If she sees you happy and relaxed...'

'And when it ends?' Still the springs snapped and, glimpsing the ending, she felt as if she were finally falling. 'What do I tell her then?'

'Relationships don't work out sometimes.' Aleksi shrugged, and then his voice was serious. He held her elbows, spoke very slowly, very clearly, because there was one thing it was imperative she understood. 'So long as you're okay, Georgie will be okay. But it *will* end, Kate. You're right about that. I don't do love. I don't do for ever.'

'You're not going to break my heart, Aleksi.' Kate's voice was firm. She almost managed condescending— only inside she didn't feel so brave, because seeing him for a few hours did enough damage to her mind. To live with him, to sleep with him, to be with him all the time with the guarantee of losing him...

She was hurting already, and he must have picked up on that.

'I'm a good lover, Kate.'

'Oh, so sex is part of the deal?'

'Of course it's not mandatory…' Aleksi said, but then he pulled apart her dressing gown.

The belt was still tight, so only her breasts were exposed, and he pulled her just a small fraction closer, not enough to be touching, but almost, *almost*, and her breasts yearned for more, instantly hardening till his skin grazed her.

'What, Kate?' His whisper was cool on her flaming cheek. 'Do you want me to say that we share a bed and don't touch? That we deny ourselves such an obvious pleasure?' He was stroking her nipple now, caressing it as he had last night, only his movements were more skilful than intuitive, driven by a goal other than lust.

She flicked his hand off. 'It's not going to happen.'

'As I was saying…' He ignored her words and lifted her onto the bench as if she was as featherlight as Lavinia, and suddenly she was at eye level with him. 'We get on, Kate, and I am a good lover. I know what to say…' he was playing with the tie of her dressing gown '…and I know how to make you happy—but you have to know that it can't last.'

'Haven't you heard a word I've said?' she demanded.

He just smiled that slightly mocking smile, and then it widened as a thought struck him.

'You're on the pill.'

'If you think—'

'I'm as clean as a whistle, Kate—had it confirmed at the hospital. I knew anyway. I always wear protection.'

'There's been no one since the hospital?'

'Actually, no!' He sounded as surprised with that fact

as Kate was. Then that devilish smile was one of the cat with the cream. 'We can play at monogamy...'

'It's all just a game to you!' She went to climb down but he held her waist.

'What's wrong with that?' Aleksi challenged. 'I play nicely...'

And then he wasn't nice at all. A skilled negotiator, Aleksi knew *exactly* when to change his tune. He dropped his hands, released the pressure and showed her a different way. 'Carry on with your life, Kate. Go and spend your weekend looking for a rental that takes pets. Oh, and in a couple of weeks you can look for work— because after all this trouble with Nina I won't be there much longer.' She could have stepped down but instead she sat. 'And don't forget to keep looking for schools for Georgie...' He mocked her with a wicked smile then. 'Only you've already found the one you want, haven't you? The offer's there, Kate. You can have everything you want for Georgie.'

'You're rushing me!'

'How?' Aleksi challenged. 'I'm not demanding a response—think about it over the weekend, let me know next week. I'm not rushing you into anything...'

He did this.

Kate had watched him work and she knew he did this.

He was both good cop and bad cop rolled into one— his words were like a relentless slap on alternate cheeks and then the confusion of a soothing palm. Only she had never been the recipient of his tactics before.

'Carry on juggling and living in dreary homes, paying someone a mortgage or rent.'

Slap.

'I'm offering a solution.'

Soothe.

'Promise yourself that you'll find Georgie a tutor in a couple of years to make up for the education she's missing…'

Slap.

'I can help you do better for Georgie.'

Soothe.

'And sex isn't part of the deal. I don't need to pay you for that.'

Slap.

'We can make love because we *want* to…'

He soothed her not with words but with his mouth, kissing her hard till she was too dizzy to think, muddling her, blurring all the edges. And then those hands were back, only lower, visiting a place they had never been, and had she had time to think she might have guessed that tenderness would be his next weapon, that his hands would gently beguile, but this was Aleksi and she'd just been soothed.

His fingers were precise, insistent, the pad of his thumb bringing her rapidly close to a place she had never shared with another, his mouth on her neck sucking her, almost bruising her, his other hand at his zipper and…

What did this man do to her?

Whatever it was—he just did.

She was putty in his warm, skilful hands.

She was strong and independent and a survivor—yet in this, only in this, she was weak and needy and it was delicious.

'Take it off.' He wanted to see her, but his hands were too busy. He felt her momentarily freeze, but he wanted this. He had only had glimpses before, and he wanted the full view now. His mouth was nuzzling her breasts, his forehead butting and pushing the fabric of her dressing gown apart, and he did not care if she was embarrassed—did not give a thought to her hang-ups about her figure. All he could think of was her, and the lush spill of flesh as she shrugged off her robe, and he was lost.

Sex for Aleksi was an escape, but this was different. He could hear the little whimpers from her throat and feel the swell of her breasts in his mouth, feel this shy, guarded woman ripple into sensual life. And he wasn't escaping—he was gone. Lost in a world that was absent from pain and the bleak abyss of confusion. He remembered her soft lips last night and he wanted her to have the same.

'Aleksi, no...'

It wasn't a no that meant yes, and it wasn't a no that meant no. It was a no that said she could never enjoy it, a no that said this was not how he could pleasure her—because, naked on her kitchen bench, she felt the world coming back into focus. She felt as big and as bulky and as shiny and red as a Russian nesting doll—until he cracked that image with his mouth, dispelled it with a flick of his tongue, and eked from her the prettier woman inside. And then he did it again, till she was back in her head and alive in her body.

It was perhaps the abstinence from medication, Aleksi concluded, that had ended his abstinence from a more basic, once frequent pleasure.

It could not be *her*, could it? For Aleksi relied on no one.

And yet...

There was no one else he would consider entering unprotected, yet he relished that thought now.

'Aleksi, please...' She wanted him as she had never wanted another. She wanted—no, needed to finally know the bliss of him inside her. Yet he wouldn't give her that satisfaction just yet.

He would give her another kind first.

Aleksi knew how to pleasure women. He had been taught, and he had listened well. God, but he'd loved those lessons. He listened to the moans and the trip of the rhythm in his lovers' breathing and there was always an unseen smile of triumph on his busy lips as he took her to the edge—except there were no mechanics in play today. Aleksi was as lost as she.

He could feel her orgasm, he could hear it and taste it, feel the beats of her climax on his lips, and there was no smile of triumph, just unadulterated satisfaction in his mind. Her pleasures were his—till a lush, greedy selfishness invaded.

And she shared in that selfishness.

The pure pleasure of an individual want that *could* be shared. Her nails dug into his shoulders, pushing him away, pulling him in, and she was writhing as he broke her open further, to reveal the prettiest of them all, to expose a Kate that she hadn't known was there.

A Kate who sobbed and begged and whimpered and relished. And still, even as she gathered herself up, even as she tried to put all the little Kates back inside themselves, he did not relent.

Oh, he dragged his mouth up her stomach to her neck, he held her as she came back to the world, but he did not abate. She was weak, and she wanted to regroup. Her head was on his shoulder now, but he pushed it back.

He smiled at her, and then he slipped down the zipper of his pants, unfurled his magnificent self—not discreetly, instead very deliberately—and she felt the startle of a starter's gun. Staring down at his glorious erection, she felt as if she were being propelled, unready, out of the gate—she wanted to slow down, to savour, to come back to the world after the decadent escape his lips had allowed her. Yet there he was.

Her boss, her dream, and now her lover.

She wanted to discuss, to think, to question—only not as much as she wanted him.

Wanted more than the shudder of an orgasm and the freedom of exploration.

He *was* beautiful.

Kisses in the dark didn't do him justice.

He was at her entrance, and she ran a finger around the tip of him, felt a helpless excitement at his rare beauty, and her own, too.

Why didn't she feel shy under such intense scrutiny?

Why was only a teeny, irrelevant part of her thinking of the slim, childless beauties he must be so much more used to?

Because his delight in her was so obvious.

He stroked his tip along her pretty, wet place and she shuddered involuntarily.

So he stroked her again and again, and let her glimpse just how good this was going to be, made her squirm with fresh want till he was sure she was more than ready.

'Please.' She was begging now. 'Aleksi, please.'

But since when did Aleksi play nice?

'All this can be yours.'

She'd never know the massive effort it took for him to step back from her, to somehow contain himself, to get himself back into his pants and pull up his zipper—but he had been ruthless at getting his own way for a very long time, and Aleksi *really* wanted things his way now.

'You—!' She didn't say it—she didn't have to. All he did was shrug.

'Let me know on Monday.' She could see the scratches

from her nails on his back as he turned and pulled on his shirt as her phone rang. 'Are you going to get that?'

She wouldn't have—except it was her sister.

And she wished—even as she heard what was said, even as she acknowledged that her sister was absolutely right to have rung—just wished the call had come ten minutes later. Because what she heard made it incredibly hard to be brave, to refuse, to turn down Aleksi's once-in-a-lifetime offer.

'It's Georgie.' As she replaced the receiver, even if she loathed him at this moment, she knew he was human. Even if she wanted to be brave for a little while longer, where Georgie was concerned she simply couldn't. 'She wet the bed, she's in tears. She didn't want to upset me.'

'About what?'

'She's being bullied.'

'Bullied?'

Kate's heart was in her throat. 'I knew she didn't fit in. I know the other children can be a bit mean to her. But they actually pinch her. They hide her glasses. They throw her lunch in the sandpit. They call her names. She just told my sister. She didn't want to tell me because she knows there's nothing I can do...'

Always—no matter how busy his day, no matter what was going on his life—always he took time to hear about Georgie. Only this morning he didn't. Instead, Kate watched as he patted the pockets of his jacket and looked for his phone—then remembered he'd thrown it away.

'I need a phone.'

'That's all you can say?' she asked, hurt beyond belief.

'I could say plenty, Kate.' Instead he took out his

chequebook and put that impossible figure into words and then seven figures, and then tore it out of the book and placed it on the table. 'But you already have the answer.'

She did.

And what mother wouldn't sell her soul for her daughter? Kate tried to reason. At least this way she wouldn't be beholden to him for years—wouldn't be dangling on a string, nervous to answer back in case he fired her, worrying for the next twelve years that he might up and relocate to Europe or...

Oh, there were many reasons to take it, but only then did it dawn on her—only then did she acknowledge what was really stopping her. Only then did the truth she had tried to deny for years hit her.

It had been easy to blame Georgie for her lack of relationships—easy to say she was too busy for romance, that she didn't want a partner invading their lives. Oh, there had been so many reasons, so many excuses, and all, in part, had been true.

Yet there was a bigger truth.

From the day Aleksi Kolovsky had stepped off the plane and run a bored eye over her swollen stomach she had been attracted to him.

From the day he had walked into the maternity ward and plucked her and Georgie from the pitying stares and the incessant beat of loneliness she had held a soft spot for him.

But more than that—oh, so much more than that.

She stared for a dangerous second into eyes that were as grey and murky as the ocean after a storm, saw the beauty and the danger and the hidden depths and the strange pull that always, always dragged her in. Then she saw the mouth that both kissed and cursed, the supreme package that was Aleksi, a man who offered her escape while warning her not to love him—except his warnings came too late. Nearly five years too late, in fact. There were no hatches left to batten down, no time for rapid preparation.

The storm that was Aleksi Kolovsky had already hit, already invaded.

It was quite possible that she already loved him.

CHAPTER SIX

'I DON'T have to go back?'

Georgie's eyes shone with a hope that had been missing for a long time. Kate had left Aleksi and driven two hours to the country where her sister Julie lived, and had broken the news to her daughter.

'I don't ever have to go back to that school?'

'No, you don't.'

It was such a relief to tell her. Oh, Kate knew running away from problems wasn't the answer, but watching her daughter struggle and struggle just to belong, watching her spark fade, wasn't the answer either.

Telling her about Aleksi was harder.

She was so accepting, so delighted, so *happy* with the news that Kate found it hard to meet her sister's eyes.

'You're a dark horse!' Julie grinned when Kate joined her in the kitchen. 'God, Kate, this is fantastic. I'm so happy for you.'

'It's early days.'

'You're getting engaged!' Julie refused to be anything less than delighted for her sister, and wrapped her in a huge embrace. 'After all you've been through, I'm just so glad to see you happy. Now, go!' Julie said. 'We'll have Georgie while you sort everything out. You go and do what you have to.'

Julie had no idea, Kate realised as she drove from her sister's, how hard those words might hit her.

'Come in.'

Aleksi was dressed casually now.

Or as casually as a Kolovsky could manage.

In black jeans and a black T-shirt, with his hair wet from a shower and his jaw unshaven, Kate realised as she stepped into his stunning home that he was also perhaps just a touch uncomfortable.

'How did Georgie take the news?' he wanted to know.

'She's delighted.' Kate struggled to keep the unhappiness from her voice; she was a willing participant in this ruse, she reminded herself. Only this *so* wasn't what she had wanted.

'I'll show you around.'

She had never been to his home, although she had sat outside it in a car a couple of times, to be brought up to speed on a few things on Aleksi's way to catch a flight.

She had never, though, been invited inside, and from what she knew few women were.

Aleksi lived outside of the city. It had always surprised her. Such an eligible bachelor should surely have penthouse city views. When he needed to be close by work, or when he brought a woman back, he used hotels. It shouldn't have surprised her, really—after all, she had once worked for Levander, who had chosen to live fulltime in a luxury hotel.

'I'm not a trauma doctor like my brother,' Aleksi had once said. 'I don't need to be three minutes' drive away from work. An emergency for me can be dealt with online.'

FREE Merchandise is 'in the Cards' for you!

Dear Reader,

We're giving away FREE MERCHANDISE!

Seriously, we'd like to reward you for reading this novel by giving you **FREE MERCHANDISE** worth over **$20**. And no purchase is necessary!

You see the Jack of Hearts sticker above? Paste that sticker in the box on the Free Merchandise Voucher inside. Return the Voucher promptly…and we'll send you valuable Free Merchandise!

Thanks again for reading one of our novels—and enjoy your Free Merchandise with our compliments!

Pam Powers

Pam Powers

P.S. Look inside to see what Free Merchandise is **"in the cards"** for you!

(H-P-01/11)

▲ If offer card is missing write to: The Reader Service, P.O. Box 1867, Buffalo, NY 14240-1867 or visit www.ReaderService.com ▲

BUSINESS REPLY MAIL

FIRST-CLASS MAIL   PERMIT NO. 717   BUFFALO, NY

POSTAGE WILL BE PAID BY ADDRESSEE

THE READER SERVICE

PO BOX 1867

BUFFALO NY 14240-9952

NO POSTAGE
NECESSARY
IF MAILED
IN THE
UNITED STATES

And so he showed her around. It was an amazing home, sun-drenched and tastefully furnished. The jarrah floors echoed her steps as she walked around. Her eyes took in the huge white sofas and the modern artwork that hadn't been purchased with a five-year-old in mind! Every room offered views of the bay, and it didn't end there—there was a pool, tennis courts, a gym, and if that didn't satisfy there was always the beach a mere step away.

'This is us.' He gave a tight smile as he indicated the master bedroom, and stood watching her cheeks burn as her eyes took in the bed that was centre stage. 'There's plenty of wardrobe space...'

Except she wasn't really worried about that!

Kate peered into the *en-suite* bathroom, to the spa and double shower, and she caught a strong scent of his cologne and an intimate glimpse into the private world of Aleksi—glass bottles and heavy brushes lined up in the control room where he prepared himself for each day. She was almost dizzy with the thought that for now she would be sharing it with him. Rather than dwell on that, she walked back through the bedroom, stepped out of the French doors and onto the decking area.

'The view's amazing.' Port Phillip Bay was a vast horseshoe that spread from Queenscliffe on one end to the sharp peaks of Melbourne's city buildings on the other, and Alexi's house sat in between, with each destination a possibility. She could see a pier nearby, and tried to hazard which one, but then she looked to the left and there was another. The water was so close she could hear it lap, lap, lap, and then swish as it pulled out.

'Do you swim in the bay?' He was standing beside her and she struggled to make light conversation.

'I prefer the pool,' he replied. He gave the view just a cursory glance. 'I suppose it is nice when it storms.'

'It's wonderful now!' Kate said, but Aleksi just shrugged.

'You get used to it.'

She'd never get used to it.

Even after the weekend, even after Georgie had been enrolled in her new school, ready to start midweek, even after Kate had been back at her desk for a little while on the Tuesday afternoon, there was still no getting used to anything—and not just for her either.

'Kate! *Kate?*' She could hear the incredulity in Nina's voice and then worse, far worse, the bitchy ring of her laughter. Aleksi's office door was slightly open, but even had it been closed, the stench of her words would have seeped through. 'Now I really have heard it all. Tell me, Aleksi, how is getting engaged to that bumbling whale with her illegitimate daughter supposed to convince the board you're serious about preserving our elite name?' Aleksi must have moved to close the door, but Nina halted him. 'If she really is joining our family, Aleksi, she may as well hear it. You could have any woman and you chose *her*—are the doctors quite sure that there is no brain damage after your accident?'

He had hated his mother for decades.

Not a door-slamming, palpable hatred, more an apathetic one that simmered away silently.

He cared so little for Nina, and with such good reason, that perhaps it would have been wiser to walk away after his father's death. Yet he had stayed and risen to the challenge of running the House of Kolovsky on the death of his father. After Levander had had enough of it, and

Iosef didn't want it at all, Aleksi had stepped up and taken control.

He liked the power, the life, the buzz.

Or he had done.

If his brain had been damaged in the accident, Aleksi was almost grateful for it—for now he could almost see.

Almost.

The ring was on her finger, Kate's possessions were in his home, she was picking up Georgie soon, and the little girl would start her new school tomorrow. The press were about to be informed but first, though—as it was in normal families, right?—he shared the news with his mother.

'The board will never buy it,' Nina scoffed.

'This isn't for the board.' Aleksi leant back in his chair. 'This is for me. Since the accident, I've realised how much Kate—'

'Oh, please.' Nina scorned. '*You*, taking on some other man's child? *You*, a parent?' Nina laughed. She just threw her head back and laughed at the very idea. 'How much are you paying her? Then again,' she mused, 'it wouldn't take much! She'd be grateful just to share your bed and get free board...'

Where *had* the apathy gone? Aleksi's formidable temper was usually saved for the boardroom, but today he stood from his chair, walked over to where his mother sat and stared at her—stared into those pale blue eyes—and the anger that usually seethed deep within him bubbled to the surface, even though Nina was too foolish to see it.

'When I had my accident,' Aleksi said slowly, 'she was there every day for me.'

'Because you *pay* her to be!'

'When I was in the Caribbean she called. She—'

'Because, like every other woman in Melbourne, she's crazy about you.' Nina was as hard as nails. 'You don't have to get engaged to the halfwit. Are you really telling me that her child is moving in too? That the slut is bringing her—'

'When I watch Kate with her daughter—' he spoke over Nina's filth, his voice slowly rising '—I see, for the first time, how a mother *should* behave.' He was standing over her now. 'I see how a parent *should* care for their child.' Then he stopped. Not a word more was uttered, not a hand raised, but he stared at his mother till she blinked with nervousness. He opened his mouth and then closed it again, because if he spoke now he would annihilate her. And maybe she sensed it, because only when he had walked back to his desk did Nina find the bravado to speak again—her voice not quite so assured now.

'If you do care for her, Aleksi, then what the hell are you doing? The press will crucify her.' Her voice was almost sympathetic. 'There will be huge interest in the engagement.'

'Kate can handle it,' Aleksi said, but though his voice was sure he himself was not. For the first time guilt was trickling in. He was more than used to the regular probes into his private life, and the girls he usually dated were delighted at any publicity—but Kate?

'What about her child?' Nina prodded again, smothering a satisfied smile as she found her son's buttons and pushed them, though he tried to hide it. 'Of course if you are in love, if this is what you want, then this is what you must do—but to bring an innocent child into the glare of publicity… Well, I hope you are very sure of your feelings for them both.'

Aleksi wasn't the only one whose heart was plummeting as Nina spoke.

Kate's shame and anger at Nina's initial reaction was now being replaced by guilt—fear, even. Because, no matter what she could deal with, she didn't want it to impact on her daughter. Yet on her way to work she had stopped at the school. Loath to cash the cheque, still not a hundred percent sure of her decision, Kate had paid the first term's tuition with the very last of her savings and bought the uniform and books with her emergency credit card. And then, when panic had again overwhelmed her, she had asked to be shown the classroom once more. The sight of it had temporarily soothed her nerves.

This was the right decision.

It was the education her daughter needed.

As Aleksi had said, relationships broke up all the time—but at least Georgie's future was secured.

'Your choice, Aleksi…'

Kate could almost see in her mind's eye Nina shrug her shoulders, and then, of course, she moved onto business.

'Have you got the Krasavitsa projections?'

'Sorry?'

'You said you'd have them.' Nina was curt. 'I want to go through them.' There was a pause, an interminable pause, and Kate sat at her desk frowning as Nina continued. 'Don't try and mess me about, Aleksi. You assured me I'd have them well in advance of the meeting…'

'One moment.'

'You do have them?'

'Of course.' He walked out his office and to her desk. She could see his pallor, and was relieved when he closed the door behind him. 'I'm sure you heard all that.'

'I couldn't exactly *not* hear,' she said dryly.

'Are you sure about this?' Aleksi looked over to her, and it was Kate's turn to be angry.

'It's a bit late for concern now, Aleksi—I've already told Georgie, and she knows she's starting her new school tomorrow. I'm picking her up from Julie's in an hour, to bring her to her new home, and all of a sudden you're concerned for us.' She glared at him. 'You promise me one thing,' she said. 'Never, to anyone, do you reveal this is a ruse.'

'I won't.' He meant it.

'Swear it, Aleksi,' Kate said. 'I'll sell myself for my daughter's sake, but she must never, ever know about it.'

'And she won't.' Aleksi said, 'We fell in love, remember?'

Somehow she felt as if he were mocking her—or rather, Kate realized, it was the impossibility of his words.

'When the time comes, we'll say we fell out of love. That when I got well I saw that perhaps the accident had made me maudlin for a while...' He gave her a smile, tried to reassure her, but she couldn't return it. 'We'll talk about this later. Right now I need the Krasavitsa projections...' He raked a hand through his hair—he still hadn't had it cut. 'I need you to get straight onto it. I'll tell Nina they're nearly ready, but you'll need to give it your immediate—'

'They're done,' Kate interrupted him, clicking a button on her computer. From behind where he stood the figures he needed started printing. 'You still need to go through them.'

'I need the original figures. Not the ones—'

'I've got them for you.' There was just the tiniest flicker of a frown on his face, but then normal services resumed and Aleksi picked up the paperwork and scanned the figures. It was Kate frowning now. 'You don't remember do you?'

He didn't answer.

'Aleksi, you don't remember her asking for these earlier...'

'Shh...' He hushed her, as he often did when concentrating, but Kate would not be silenced. There had been too many small things he'd missed—too many details that could no longer be glossed over.

'I'll be going home, then.' As she stood, only then did he look up. 'I want to oversee the removalists.'

'When will you be back?'

'Should I really come back to work?' Kate's eyes were wide. 'I'm supposed to be your fiancée.'

'You know I need you here.'

'You don't remember her asking, do you?' Kate asked again, and she saw him swallow, saw his eyes dart to the door to check that it was closed. 'You don't remember Nina asking for those figures.'

'Of course I do,' he said, giving her a scornful look.

He could never admit it.

Never.

Not once had he admitted to any weakness, and now, when he most needed to be strong...

'Aleksi?' Her eyes were worried. 'Your hair needs a cut.'

'I'm busy.'

'Every fortnight, without fail—'

'It suits me longer,' he said, daring her to contradict him.

'Since when,' Kate said, walking over, taking one of his hands, 'did you cut your own nails?' He withdrew his hand and she wondered if she was right. Yes, his hair was just a touch longer, and, yes, he had been phenomenally busy last week—too busy perhaps for a manicure? Yet this was Aleksi Kolovsky...

He never forgot, never missed an appointment at the salon. He made everyone else look scruffy with his fastidiousness. No one looking at this elegant coiffed man would see a hair out of place, would see him as anything other than utterly and completely in control.

Except she loved him—maybe.

Which meant *she* noticed.

'They can't know. The board can't know.' Aleksi voice was hoarse. 'My mother—it would be like blood in the water. They'd feed like sharks...'

'She will know soon,' Kate said, because after all surely his mother loved him, too?

'She mustn't.'

'What's wrong, Aleksi?'

He hated this revelation—hated standing in front of her and admitting...what? That there was a flaw in his armour and he couldn't bear it? He couldn't stand weakness, abhorred it, so he silenced her, pressed his mouth to hers and did what he still did brilliantly—because this he could never, ever forget how to do.

This made it possible.

His mouth, his taste, his scent, his maleness pressing into her, chased all the fears and doubts away.

As his tongue played with hers, as his animal magnetism drew her into him, the impossible was made easy.

He obliterated doubt with one stroke of his tongue.

She must not care, must brace herself for walking away, but while she stayed *this* made it do-able—his kiss, his touch, the only things that made sense.

His fingers were in her hair, his hands insistent, and then they moved down over her back to caress her hips.

He made her both weak and strong. Strong because he made anything possible, and weak because he could take her any time he wanted.

His erection wedged into her groin and she gasped into his mouth.

'Aleksi, how long…?' Nina opened the door of his office, her voice trailing off as she caught her son in a passionate clinch. But she was the mother of Kolovsky sons, and had long got over any embarrassment. 'I need those papers,' she said, as Aleksi released Kate from his potent grip. 'Assuming, of course, that you have them.' Her eyes held just a fraction of challenge, and Kate felt sure that Nina knew there was something amiss with her son.

'Here.' Normally he would never have handed them over without checking them carefully first, but Aleksi reassured himself that Kate had prepared them so he trusted they were right.

And then he quickly checked them himself.

He trusted no one.

'You haven't signed them off,' Nina said. 'I'm not going to work on figures that you haven't approved. Here…' She headed to Kate's desk and picked up a pen, which Aleksi had no choice but to take. After just a beat of a pause, he signed off the figures with his usual flourish.

Nina caught Kate's eye. 'We will dine tonight…' She gave Kate a smile that didn't meet her eyes. 'To celebrate.'

'It's Georgie's first night in her new home. I really don't want to take her out,' Kate replied.

'You don't bring children to dinner! Ring the nanny agency.' She took the forms from Aleksi and without another word headed out.

'That should keep her quiet for a while,' Aleksi said, once she was safely out of earshot.

'It's lucky that I had them on the computer.' Kate said, but her voice was far from even. The thought of getting a stranger to look after Georgie had her in a spin. Only now was the true reality of being a part of the Kolovsky world starting to hit home. But her thoughts were side-swiped as Aleksi responded to her comment.

'I meant,' he drawled, 'the kiss.'

It would have been kinder to Kate had he simply slapped her.

CHAPTER SEVEN

'SHE'LL be fine,' Aleksi said with a sigh, as for the third time in as many minutes Kate questioned whether they really had to go out. 'The whole point of this exercise is that we are seen.'

'It's her first night here,' Kate pointed out, although Georgie really did seem fine.

Even though she had only met Aleksi perhaps a handful of times, when Kate had had to come in at weekends or in the evenings and had had no choice but to bring her, he had always been lovely to Georgie, and Georgie, in turn, thought he was fantastic.

Of course Kate had played it all down as she'd shown her daughter around her new home. Yes, Aleksi was her boyfriend, she'd told Georgie. It wasn't a complete lie—she was, after all, crazy about him. He filled her every waking thought and then came back for a nightly visit to her dreams, and as of tonight she'd be sleeping beside him.

'Will you get married?' Georgie had asked, and only then had it tipped into a lie. Because, like love, marriage for Aleksi was something that would never happen.

'Let's just see how we all get on together first.'

'But he's bought you a ring...' Georgie's eyes fell on the emerald-cut diamond that alone could pay for her education and beyond. 'That means you're going to get married.'

There was no easy answer to logic combined with a five-year-old's dreams of how the world should be, so Kate had stayed silent, and now Georgie was playing on the tennis court with Sophie, her new nanny, shrieking with laughter as she patted back balls while Kate prepared herself for a glittering night with the Kolovsky family.

A night out she didn't want.

'I thought the exercise was to show how responsible the new Aleksi was,' Kate said, still hoping for a last-minute reprieve.

'Which is why I've paid for a top nanny who's going to play games and have fun with her.' Aleksi clearly didn't see what the problem was. 'Hell, we'll only be a couple of hours. The last thing I want is a prolonged night with my family.' He was knotting his tie. Backwards and forwards he slid the silk through the knot, then cursed in frustration as with each attempt it fell apart.

'Do you want a hand?'

'I don't need you to dress me,' Aleksi hissed.

Kate bit her tongue, because she knew he was in pain. Knew because since that night he hadn't taken a single painkiller. But it was more than that. Since the office, since Nina's cruel observations, his mood had been black. So much for a warm welcome to their new home!

And so much for sensitivity. When she was sliding on her dress and struggling with the zip Aleksi turned around. 'You can't wear that.'

'Excuse me?'

'You wore that at last year's Christmas party.'

'Should I be touched that you remember?'

'I remember,' Aleksi said, walking over, 'because you had the tag hanging out at the back all night—just as you have now.' He flicked it with distaste. 'My real fiancée would not shop at a high street store.'

'And no doubt your *real* fiancée wouldn't have this dress size,' Kate said sharply, mortified as she tucked in the label. 'I must have forgotten to pack my designer wardrobe.'

'Buy one!' Aleksi said. 'I gave you a more than generous allowance…' Then his eyes narrowed. 'I suppose you're saving that for your nest egg.'

'It just doesn't feel right,' she admitted, 'cashing the cheque…'

'So you're doing this for nothing?' Aleksi gave her a wide-eyed look. 'You're here simply out of the goodness of your heart?'

She'd seen him so often like this at work, with his family—never once had it been aimed at her.

'Tomorrow Nikita will sort out your wardrobe—she is the top designer at Kolovsky.' He watched in exasperation as she used the tongs in her hair. 'Why the hell didn't you get someone in to do that? You know what to do—you know how to prepare…'

Yes, she did.

For Alexi's dates Kate would often organise the hairdresser, the beautician, the day spa. Which would all have been rather lovely for her—except Aleksi's usual dates didn't generally have a nanny to interview. Despite the fact Aleksi had said an interview was unnecessary. Nor did they have an almost five-year-old who wanted her mum to sit with her while she had dinner, and to spend a little while exploring her new home.

So instead she'd had to make do with a fifteen-minute

make-over to transform her from drab to almost fab—well, perhaps not by Kolovsky standards. As a single mum Kate was rather used to performing great feats in record time—she did it each morning, after all, just to get to work. Now she slicked on foundation, dotted her cheeks with blush, and attempted massive renovations on her eyes.

Aleksi watched, his impatience mounting with each passing minute.

He'd finally knotted his tie.

His hair, even though it might require a cut, fell into exquisite shape, and he slapped on some cologne and tried not to think about the snakepit he was exposing her to tonight. Wished he had thought and had packed her off for a makeover—the press would be there, his mother would make sure of that, and Kate, with her high street dress and homemade hairdo, would cause a frenzy.

'A little empathy would be nice.' She glared at him as she stuffed lipstick and mints and a mobile phone into her evening bag. 'And before you tell me to buy myself some from the generous allowance you're giving me, I'm not talking about a perfume!'

'You've got a run in your stockings.' Aleksi pointed out, then stood there, lips pursed, as she took off her high shoes, ripped off her stockings and replaced her shoes.

'What?' Kate flashed. 'Am I supposed to whip out a spare pair?' Aleksi said nothing, but Kate was on a roll. 'Are my calves too pale to be seen out with you?'

He didn't like this grown-up game.

Didn't like watching her kiss Georgie goodnight and seeing how she left her mobile number *and* the restaurant number on the bench in the kitchen, because Aleksi's silver fridge didn't possess a single magnet. Didn't like her assurance to Sophie that they'd be home well before midnight.

It had never been a factor for Aleksi before.

She could feel his tension as the driver pulled into the restaurant. She wasn't particularly surprised by it—after all, she had arranged a few family get-togethers in her time as both Levander's and Aleksi's PA, and neither brother had particularly embraced them.

This was different, though, and as the car pulled up, as she saw the throng of photographers waiting to greet them, Kate's nerves, which seemed to have been placed in temporary cold storage while she had dealt with the practicalities of Georgie and moving house, suddenly rapidly thawed and caught up.

This might be a charade for her and Aleksi, but for tonight, and for the next couple of months, this was real to everyone else.

This was her life.

And now, when she thought she might turn tail and run, he took her hand and moved in to speak quietly into the shell of her ear.

'You're going to be fine,' Aleksi soothed, his fingers smoothing a stray curl behind her ear. 'You look wonderful...'

And then he kissed her—except it tasted of deceit, and Kate wasn't stupid enough to believe his words were for her, that those tender gestures weren't for the cameras that were exploding outside the car, and she pulled away.

'It would have been nice...' she leant back in his arms, smiled into his eyes for the cameras and then spoke her truth '...if you could have said all this back at the house.'

'I thought it.' Aleksi didn't bat an eyelid, just smiled and played with her hair and lived the lie so well. 'Now I say it.'

As they stepped out, whether it was for the cameras' benefit or not, she was pathetically grateful for his arm around her shoulders as they walked the short but daunting distance to the restaurant. Kate never liked having her photo taken at the best of times, and right now it was possibly the worst of times as by happy manufactured coincidence Nina's car arrived just a moment behind them. She realised she was to greet her supposed future mother-in-law in front of the full glare of the press.

'So that was the delay in the car,' Kate turned and whispered in his ear. 'Aleksi, remind me again to never believe anything you say or do.'

He laughed—for the first time in a very long time, Aleksi laughed. There was no fooling Kate, and it was actually refreshing. He was also curiously proud of his fake fiancée as she handled Nina with far more aplomb than most could muster.

'Darling Kate!' Nina was at her false best, commandeering Kate as if she had missed her all her life, air-kissing and cooing. Kate played the game too, even accepting the other woman's bony arm in hers as they were guided into the restaurant. Now, surely she should breathe—except the waiter was leading them through the safety of the packed restaurant, not to some exclusive, secluded corner, but back outside to the street they had just left.

'It's such a nice night.' Nina smiled maliciously. 'I thought we should eat outside. Don't be shy,' she chided Kate, 'it's just a few cameras—the world wants to see the young lovers...'

They were seated. Despite the short notice, Nina had

done well. There were a couple of aunts, Iosef was there with his wife Annie, and also the beautiful Kolovsky daughter, Annika, with her handsome husband, Ross.

It hurt to watch. For Kate it actually hurt to watch the way they pored over the menu, the way the private conversation continued despite the crowd—and the way Ross held Annika's hand the whole way through.

Love couldn't be manufactured and faked for the cameras, she thought with a flutter of panic, sipping her champagne, feeling every eye on her, and most of all feeling Nina just waiting for her to slip up. What mother would want to turn on her own son? Kate tried to fathom as Aleksi spoke with Ross, his new brother-in-law. What mother would so badly try to expose her son's faults for the sake of winning?

'What's wrong, Kate?' Nina asked pointedly. 'You look uncomfortable.'

She couldn't do this, Kate realized. She couldn't sit and be demure and plastic—even if she was a fake fiancée she was still herself, and for this charade to continue that was who she needed to be.

'I am uncomfortable,' Kate said, and the table fell silent. 'It must be the coat hanger I forgot to take out of my skirt.'

It was nice to see Nina's face falter for a second, but nicer—far, far nicer—was once again the rare sound of Aleksi's laughter, the feel of his hot hand closing around hers as he addressed his mother.

'See now why I love her?'

He didn't, of course, Kate told herself, reminded herself, insisted to herself, over and over again. Only now she was herself, now she was being who she really was, the night and the table were more lively. Even Iosef and Annie seemed a touch reluctant when Iosef's pager urgently sounded and they duly made their excuses.

'One of the benefits of being a doctor,' Aleksi remarked quietly, as he said goodnight to his brother and sister-in-law.

'Had I known it would be such a good night,' Iosef murmured to his twin, 'I would have arranged at least another hour.' He turned to Kate. 'It really has been nice meeting you.'

It was strange, Kate pondered, to kiss the cheek of a man who looked exactly like Aleksi, to smile and chat, to look into the same slate-grey eyes and yet feel nothing.

She almost wished she could ask them to swap—so she could get through this without emotion. Because one touch from Aleksi and her heart was on skid row.

Aleksi had dreaded this night, and no doubt would regret it in the morning, when the press did their savage best to mock the reunion and ridicule Kate, but to his absolute surprise he was enjoying himself in a way he never had with his family.

Oh, his mother was at her most irritating and caustic, but he was so proud of how Kate had just shrugged and carried on. There was no need to impress, he realized. She had this confidence, this strength that amazed him—a side to her he had never seen or appreciated before.

For the first time he was actually enjoying an evening with his family, and even Annika seemed to be relaxing—until Nina introduced a new subject. 'I hear you are going to the UK,' she said to Aleksi, 'to try and dissuade Belenki.'

'I'm not just going to see him.' Aleksi didn't even look over to his mother as he spoke. 'I would like to meet Riminic, my new nephew...' Now he looked over to Nina and watched her face pale, watched as she reached for a glass of water.

'His name is Dimitri,' Nina croaked.

'My mistake,' Aleksi said. 'Are you going over to meet your new grandson?' he asked. 'Or doesn't a Detsky Dom orphanage boy count?'

'It's too soon.' Nina was having great trouble wearing her false smile, and all the aunts were sitting in rigid silence, awaiting her response. 'Levander and Millie said they don't want him to be crowded, that they don't want too much fuss made.'

'Well, you'll never be guilty of that.'

'Aleksi's an expert in children suddenly.' Nina smiled to the table. 'Next time you must bring along Georgie. We'd all love to meet her.'

You could have heard a pin drop.

'You've got a child?' It was Ross, Annika's husband, who broke the silence.

'Georgie.' Kate nodded.

'How old?' Annika's voice was curiously high.

'She's nearly five.'

'A lovely age.' Nina smiled falsely. 'She'll be thrilled that Mummy's engaged, no doubt—what little girl doesn't harbour the dream of being bridesmaid?'

'Aleksi...' Annika and Ross were ready to leave now; the night was wrapping up. 'Can I have a word?'

Of all his family, it was Annika he was closest to. He knew how hard things had been for her, the expectations that had been placed on her slender shoulders and how hard it must have been to turn her back on them. She was, to Nina's horror, finishing her nursing training, and was hoping to specialise in aged care—she amazed him too. Every day she grew stronger. Out of her family's clutches and in Ross's arms she grew stronger by the minute.

'Of course.'

'Away from…' Annika looked uncomfortable and frowned to Ross, who quickly flicked his eyes away. Aleksi's heart sank, and he shot Ross a black look for his betrayal.

He had been dreading this day.

Ross, a doctor, had seen Aleksi's X-Rays, showing old injuries, when he had been admitted to the hospital after the car crash—had confronted him about them. In a moment of weakness, and also to assure him that Annika hadn't suffered the same treatment from their father, Aleksi had confessed that he had been beaten in the past. Ross had promised never to reveal what he had said.

'Ross had no right!' Aleksi flared when they were out of earshot. 'I don't care if he's your husband—I hope his medical malpractice insurance—'

'What are you talking about, Aleksi?' Annika frowned. 'He's just worried—*I'm* worried.' She swallowed. 'Kate's got a daughter.'

'Georgie.' Aleksi nodded, relief whooshing through him. He kicked himself for overreacting, but he had been so sure Ross had revealed his past.

'When Mum rang…' Annika was clearly uncomfortable '…she said you were pulling some stunt but that we should be seen to be supportive. Look, I get that there are a lot of people you have to convince you are settling down, and I have no idea what Mum's up to, pretending to support you…'

'Don't worry about Kate and me.'

'I'm not.' She looked squarely at him. 'Kate seems lovely. She seems more than capable. If you are genuinely engaged then I couldn't be more delighted for you. If you're not…'

'Kate and I have worked together a long time,' Aleksi said. 'Only when I was injured did we realize—'

'Save it for the press,' Annika hissed, clearly not convinced. 'What I am saying is that if you two are just doing this to appease the board, if this is just some convenient arrangement... She has a *child*, Aleksi!'

'I am looking after Georgie,' he protested.

'So it's about the money for Kate, then?' Annika asked cynically.

'You don't know what you're talking about.'

'I know this much,' Annika flared, and Aleksi realised just how strongly his sister felt. 'If it's anything other than love guiding this, then you two had better think long and hard about Georgie. Do you really want a child caught up in all this? The press will give you both absolute hell if it comes out. Do you really want all this to land on a five-year-old?'

'She's sensible for her age,' he said defensively, although his heart was sinking with every sentence she uttered.

'Oh, so that's okay, then,' Annika sneered, and then her voice broke. 'She'll love you, too, Aleksi.'

'Annika—'

'No!' She would not be silenced. 'What little girl doesn't want a daddy? What little girl doesn't want to see her mum happy and live in a beautiful house?' She shook her head at her brother. 'I've seen Kate looking at you. She's crazy about you, Aleksi, but that's her problem. Just don't break that little girl's heart, too.'

He had dismissed it when his mother had said it, but hearing Annika's raw plea had Aleksi more than uneasy. He looked over to where Kate sat, smiling, chatting, making light work of his mother, and he knew, as he had always known deep down, that Kate had feelings for him. So many women had. And then she turned around, caught his eye, and she smiled a smile that was just for him.

A smile that said, *Get me out of here*.

An intimate smile that was only passed between lovers.

He would hurt her.

Of that Aleksi was in no doubt—and now here was Annika, telling him that he would hurt Georgie, too.

'Be very careful,' Annika warned, only Aleksi wasn't listening. For him the night was over.

He summoned Kate and they were out of there, the cameras clicking again, Kate once again attempting to duck his kiss as they slipped into the back seat.

'We're supposed to be unable to keep our hands off each other,' Aleksi reminded her, but even as she tried to close her eyes and think of Kolovsky all she could see was the cheque still in her bag, waiting to be cashed.

She felt paid for.

'It's like kissing an aunt.' Aleksi gave in and brooded instead, sat drumming his fingers on the passenger door as they were driven back to his home.

But worse, far worse for Aleksi, was when they arrived home. All he wanted was to take her upstairs to drive out the warnings, to convince himself they were right to be doing what they were doing, to forget for just a little while that this was a dangerous game. As if sent to remind him, as they stepped into the hall Georgie stood at the top of the stairs, a teddy on her nightdress, her hair a mass of ringlets, and a very sorry nanny by her side.

'She wouldn't go to sleep till she knew you were home.'

'She's probably a little unsettled,' Kate said as Georgie came running down the stairs.

Georgie quickly corrected her mother—she wasn't unsettled; on the contrary she was absolutely *delighted* with her new home.

'We had supper by the pool and then we took Bruce for a walk on the beach.' She was chattering so fast she could hardly get the words out in order. 'There are hundreds of different channels on Aleksi's television; I saw you arriving at the dinner and they were talking about the wedding!'

'What was she doing watching the news?' Aleksi frowned to Sophie.

'It was just for a second. She was working out the remote…'

'She is not just to be plonked in front of the television—'

'Aleksi,' Kate broke in, 'I let her watch some. It's no big deal…'

'She's not even five yet,' Aleksi warned the nanny. 'She is not to watch the news.'

'Of course, Mr Kolovsky.' Sophie's face was purple with embarrassment. 'Come on, Georgie, let's get you to bed.'

'I'll take her,' Kate said, because that was what she wanted.

It was a thoroughly over-excited Georgie that she put to bed, and it took for ever to get her to settle. Her new school uniform was hanging on the wardrobe door, as per Georgie's instructions, and she would have worn it to bed had Kate allowed it.

'I love it here,' Georgie whispered as Kate finally flicked the light off. 'Are you happy too?'

'Of course,' Kate said, and closing the bedroom door she let out a long breath, before walking along the hall to the bedroom, bracing herself to earn her keep.

'How is she?'

His suit lay in a puddle on the floor, and he lay in the bed. He didn't look up from scrolling through messages on his phone, and Kate felt suddenly shy.

She had never actually undressed in front of him. Usually, it just...well, happened. But now she stood in his vast bedroom, the bedside lights seemed to be blazing and because when packing she'd realised she truly couldn't bring *that*, her familiar tatty dressing gown was in a bin somewhere. Despite their previous intimacies, Kate just wasn't ready to undress in front of him, so instead she padded into the *en-suite* bathroom.

Her hair, of course, was everywhere. Her mascara was smudged beneath her eyes, her lipstick, despite the packaging's promise, had long, long since faded, and yet...

Her usually self-critical eyes blinked—because though she could see her faults there was something new there, something that had been missing too long. He had awoken something in her—intangible, yet somehow visible.

There was a glow that had been missing—a ripeness, a lushness, that she couldn't logically explain. As she peeled off her clothes and stepped on his scales they gave her the same old bad news—said it out loud, actually, and Kate jumped off in horror, hoping to God that Aleksi hadn't heard!

What to wear?

She stared at the neatly folded white towels that had been replaced since her shower this evening. There were bathrobes hanging against the door, as anonymous as in any hotel.

She was too nervous to go out there, so she lingered in brushing her teeth and taking off her make-up. Always till now their passion had been spontaneous, a wave that swept them up, only now she felt as if she were standing at the edge of Aleksi's glittering pool, nervous about just plunging in.

What to wear?

The question plagued her again. She didn't own a nightdress. The last time she had worn one was when Georgie had been born. Yes, she could put on a bathrobe, and then take it off when she got to bed. Brave, nervous, she opened the bathroom door. The overhead lights were off, but the dim bedside lights might just as well have been spotlights tracking her as she padded towards him, her body a contrary jumble of emotions, because she wanted him...so badly she wanted him...

Just not like this.

The French windows were open and she could hear the slow lap of the bay, except it didn't calm her a jot. She could feel his eyes on her as reached the bed and stood there.

'Are you going to wear your bathrobe to bed?'

She bit down on her lip and took it off in one fumbled motion that included lifting the sheet and sliding into bed.

She could smell his maleness, could feel his brooding mood, and she longed for the spontaneity of before—for touches that just happened, not this manufactured simulation they had invented.

His kiss was skilled and practised, his hands insistent and probing, and she tried to tell herself she enjoyed it— tried to remind her body how just a few days ago it had craved this moment, had yearned for the weight of his body and the scratch of his thigh as he parted her legs. But her body refused to listen.

Oh, she kissed him back, moaned and made noises,

but Aleksi had tasted the real Kate and knew he was getting a poor imitation of the woman he had so recently reduced to delicious begging.

And Aleksi was too proud to take favours.

'You're tired.' He rolled away from her.

'Yes.'

'It's been a long day,' Aleksi offered, and flicked off the bedside light.

'Yes.' She stared at the darkness, relieved and yet disappointed at the same time.

'They're in the bathroom cupboard, by the way,' Aleksi said, shifting onto his side to face away from her, and Kate closed her eyes at what came next. 'The headache tablets—no doubt you'll soon say you've got one.'

CHAPTER EIGHT

Krasavitsa Kate

Aleksi stared at the headline, and then at the photo.

Always the papers crucified his dates. The sleekest, glossiest were caught mid-blink or at an unflattering angle, the write-ups were always scathing—all night he had dreaded Kate's face when she saw the cruel words and pictures at the breakfast table.

And yet here she was. On the front cover.

One strap of her dress falling slightly from her shoulder, her hair rippling down the other one, her head thrown back mid-laugh, her cleavage, her arms, her flesh so refreshing—but most surprising for Aleksi next to her was himself, and for once he was smiling. Not smirking, not grinning, but there *was* a smile on his usually stern features. As he stared at the photo he tried to recall that moment, what it was that had made Kate laugh, what it was that had made him smile—only, unusually, he couldn't narrow it down to one time.

Despite the tense atmosphere, despite the barbs and the comments and the claustrophobic air any family reunion of his usually fostered, last night there had also been moments like these.

Many of them.

'There's Mummy!' A smiling face peered over not his shoulder but his elbow. 'What's that word?'

'*Krasavitsa*,' Aleksi said. 'It means beautiful woman.'

'Well, I'm not feeling so *krasavitsa* this morning!' Kate headed for the kitchen bench to pour a coffee then, realising there was no need, instead walked over to the breakfast table, where the maid was pouring it for her. The table was positioned in a sun-drenched area, over-looking the pool and the tennis courts, the French doors were open, and as she sat before the generous feast, Kate wondered how he did it. Not a single fly buzzed around the pastries and spreads—no doubt Aleksi employed someone to ward them off from a suitable distance.

She couldn't meet his eyes so she concentrated on her breakfast, choosing some lovely fresh fruit and won-dering if she should treat the next two months as some kind of mini-health retreat—swimming each day, eating all the right things. She'd come out of this all glossy and gorgeous, even if she was lugging around a broken heart.

'When you marry my mum—' Georgie's words hauled her from her introspection '—will I be a brides-maid?'

Horrified, she looked over to Aleksi, wondering what his scathing response would be, but Aleksi just smiled into his newspaper.

'Georgie…' It was Kate who answered. 'I told you—we're just seeing how things work out.' Her eyes were urgent as they darted to Aleksi's, hoping he would under-stand that marriage wasn't on Kate's agenda, but that she couldn't include her daughter in the charade and expect her not to voice the truth.

'I know that,' Georgie said, making puddles of milk on the table as she ate her cereal. 'Okay.' She looked again at Aleksi and rephrased her question. '*If* you marry my mum—will I be a bridesmaid'?'

Oh, God, she could feel every follicle on her head jump. Her teaspoon rattled against her cup as she stirred her coffee and, worse, she could feel the sting of tears, too.

Georgie was so happy, so accepting, so trusting—and it was her own mother who was setting her up for this hurt.

'I am quite sure,' Aleksi said, his voice kind because it was Georgie asking, 'that when your mother marries you will be her absolute first choice as a bridesmaid.'

Delighted with his response, Georgie finished her breakfast and scampered off to put on her new uniform as Kate sat with the unfamiliar feeling of not having to scramble together a lunch box—it was already packed and in Georgie's bag, Sophie informed her, and then she headed out to her little charge, which left Kate and Aleksi alone.

'I've been thoughtless.'

Kate frowned. Aleksi was never thoughtless—arrogant, perhaps, rude, often, but his words were never without thought.

'I am used to…' He shrugged as he tried to locate the word, except there wasn't just one. 'I'm not used to being with someone who has other things to think about.'

'Other things apart from you, you mean!' Kate tossed back, and when he smiled she couldn't help just a little one too.

'I am usually the sole focus,' he admitted. 'You have moved home, changed your daughter's school, dealt with your family, with mine, with your daughter and all the changes she is going through…' Kate blinked at this rare glimpse of sensitivity. 'It is no wonder you *were* tired last night.' And then she realised he wasn't being sensitive. He was about to more clearly spell out the rules. 'So you need to take things more easy—don't worry about going into work.'

'I'm not to work?' she gasped.

'You're my fiancée. You can hardly be my PA too.'

'I thought you *needed* me working!'

Aleksi closed his eyes for a brief second. He did not like being argued with, but more than that he didn't want to examine the truth behind what he was saying—that he might more simply just need *her*.

'My needs are more basic than that, Kate,' he settled for saying instead. 'You need some time to get used to your new surroundings, to concentrate on Georgie, make sure she is settling in okay.' He glanced at the bathrobe. 'To sort out your wardrobe and to get some rest.'

She looked away, blushing at his innuendo but Aleksi hadn't finished yet.

'Oh, and Kate…' He waited and he waited and he waited, until finally she looked at him. He wanted to ensure he had her full attention as he addressed a pertinent point. 'You haven't banked that cheque.'

She felt a blush spread over her cheeks. 'I meant to,' she said. 'I'll do it today.'

'Good,' he clipped, and then she frowned, because he smiled.

A real smile.

Only it wasn't for her.

'Wish me luck!' Georgie stood beaming in her new shoes and school uniform and little straw hat.

'You don't need luck,' Aleksi told her. 'You're going to have a great day in your new school. But good luck anyway.'

'Do you think they'll like me?' Georgie checked with Aleksi as Kate sorted out her socks, that were already slipping.

'Do *you* like you?' Aleksi asked.

'Yes!' Georgie laughed.

'Then you've got a friend already.'

It was times like that, Kate thought as she and Georgie were driven to school, when it would be so easy to love him—except that wasn't allowed in their rules.

Still, if ever she had doubted as to whether what they were doing was right, Kate had some confirmation that morning that they were.

Oh, it was all new, and of course Georgie's little classmates were curious about her, but there was a different air to the place—a feeling of rightness as Georgie proudly showed off her pencil case contents to the little girl sitting next to her, who did the same.

'She'll fit right in,' Mrs Heath, her new teacher, assured Kate. 'Go home and don't worry.'

And she would have done that—except just as she felt she could breathe and didn't feel like bursting into tears there was something new to worry about. Two vertical lines appeared between her eyes as she crossed the playground, reading the unexpected text she'd just received.

Can we meet—need to talk.
Say hi to Georgie from me.

And then, even as she erased it, another text pinged in.

As soon as you can. Really do need to speak with you.

She rang Craig straight back. 'There's not much to say!'

'Kate, just listen.'

'No, *you* listen.' She was beyond furious with Georgie's father as she stalked towards her driver. 'Not a single word from you for months and now you want to talk!'

'I read in the paper about you and Kolovsky,' Craig said. 'I'm pleased for you, Kate, it's just…'

'Just what?'

'I can't say this on the phone.'

'Then it can't be said,' Kate responded curtly, then ended the call and turned off her phone.

'Everything okay?' Phillip, her driver, checked.

'It's fine,' Kate said, then forced a smile. 'It's early days yet, but she seems really happy to be there.'

Craig wasn't going to spoil it, Kate swore to herself. If it was money he was after—and when *hadn't* he needed a loan?—then he'd better not be holding his breath.

She was doing this for Georgie.

Not Craig, not Aleksi. She was doing it for *Georgie*.

And maybe, Kate conceded, she was also doing this for herself—though not for the money.

She was, Kate realised, buying a little bit of time with Aleksi, for herself.

It should have been a relief not to work.

She *was* tired.

And not just from the whirlwind that had taken place in her life in the past few days.

As the days ticked by, and her stomach turned from paper-white to lobster-pink, to honey-brown as she lay on the lounger between trips to boutiques and beauticians, it was, Kate reflected, no wonder she'd spent the last few years feeling permanently exhausted.

It took three full-time staff and one part-time person, on top of Aleksi's regular crew, to perform all that she routinely had.

Sophie sorted out books and clothes and homework and readers and, concerned about her charge's love for processed cheese and juice boxes, bizarrely spent entire mornings while Georgie was at school sculpting carrots into mini-carrots and celery into mini-celery and making heart and star-shaped ice cubes to liven up the water for Georgie's after-school snack!

Bruce was returned unrecognisable from the groomers. Shampooed, washed and clipped, he was walked twice a day by Kate's occasional driver, but lay mainly dozing and scented on the decking as Kate tried to summon the energy to flop into the pool.

And, of course, with a child in the house an extra cleaner was employed.

Yes, the days were full of pampering and indulgences—like catching up on the pile of books she had meant to read. But there was only so many treatments at the day spa and only so much lounging one could do.

The afternoons were the most wonderful.

She always waiting at the school gates for Georgie—even though Sophie thought it was her job. Kate could never willingly miss the sight of her daughter in a sea of children, smiling, laughing as she came out at the end of the day, once even waving a party invitation. It was so nice to take ages over her reader, to go for a walk on the beach together.

It was the nights that were hell.

Last night they'd been out to dinner, holding hands across the table, with a kiss for the cameras, but then, after a blistering row, when she really had had a head-ache, Aleksi had stormed off to the city and spent the night in a hotel—at least that was what she'd hopelessly assumed. Now he was back, had taken the afternoon off work, and was in the blackest of moods.

He thumped balls over the net as she lay on the loung-er trying to relax, trying not to turn on her phone and see if Craig had called *again*. Kate knew she was a bit of a poor excuse for a bought and paid for fiancée—to Aleksi's intense annoyance she jumped out of her skin every time he came near her. It was her mind that didn't want this, battling with her body that so desperately did. No, she was a very poor excuse because, despite her ex-tremely pressing finances and having already received a bill from the school for next term's fees, she still hadn't cashed his cheque.

He really was pounding those tennis balls; every time the machine slammed one out he slammed it back—slicing his shots, brimming with suppressed rage.

Long-limbed, his black hair shiny with sweat, his top off, he was incredibly beautiful, Kate thought, hiding her wistful expression behind dark glasses. Thanks to his time recuperating in the West Indies his hospital pallor had long since dimmed, and the wasting on his leg was diminishing rapidly with his punishing exercise sched-ule. If she didn't know better—if she didn't lie beside him at night and feel him tense in pain, hear him swim at three a.m. just to ease the cramping—then she'd think he looked a picture of health.

If you ignored the black rings beneath his eyes and the tension etched in his features, the dangerous energy to him that wasn't abating… Kate was sure it wasn't just the lack of action in the bedroom that was fuelling him.

Belenki was still permanently unavailable when

Aleksi tried to communicate with him, and Aleksi wasn't a man used to being left on hold. Add to that the takeover bid against him, and Kate somehow knew there wasn't enough tennis balls on the planet to quell what was fuelling his anger.

He was walking towards her now, barely limping, yet it must surely be an effort. His breath was hard from exertion, his naked chest rising, and he fixed her with a smile that didn't reassure her in the slightest. Then he lowered his head, his mouth hard on hers. His skin was hot but his mouth was cool, and she closed her eyes—not from passion but to try to blot the tears. Because she had seen the glint of a camera lens too, and knew this display of affection was only for them.

'I think they just got their picture,' she whispered.

'Then let's give them another.' He dragged a chair over with his foot and sat opposite her, toying with the tie on her sarong.

'Please don't…' She closed her eyes in shame at the thought of being exposed in just her bikini in the paper.

'Why not?' Still he fiddled with the tie on her sarong, and she struggled to find her voice.

Her mind was not on the cameras now, but on his hand, his palm grazing her nipple, which was thick and swollen. She wished it were different. She hated her body—hated its passionate responses to him, hated that even after a passionless, manufactured kiss still she flared for him.

'Maybe I don't want to be made a fool of. Where were you last night?' She reached for his hand and removed it.

'Don't question me,' he ground out.

'Then don't expect me on tap,' she snapped back.

'Hardly!' came his sarcastic reply, and still he played with the knot.

'Maybe *krasavitsa* Kate doesn't want to read about her fiancé's indiscretions in the paper.' She took a deep breath. 'You're going to publicly dump me anyway once this is over, once you've convinced the board you're respectable.'

'Leave it.' He could not think about then. Could not stand to think about the day when all this would be over—when everything he had would perhaps be gone. When nothing remained, when she knew his shame, she would hate him too. He looked into her troubled blue eyes and he was angry. Because she knew nothing—none of them, not one of them, knew the danger, knew the trouble. He carried it all…

'In a couple of months,' she persisted, but her voice was strangled when he finally undid the knot, her hand reaching to close together the flimsy material. 'Please don't, Aleksi.'

'I would be forgiven for straying,' he said nastily. 'As all we do is kiss, and always you are covered to the neck.'

'Sorry I'm not as blatant as your usual scrubbers,' she hissed.

'Take it off,' Aleksi demanded, his voice silken, his mouth soft. But he was the smiling assassin, and she sat there, shivering in her own misery. It wasn't the camera she feared, wasn't her cottage cheese thigh on the cover of a magazine, but his scrutiny, his distaste she dreaded right now. 'It's warm; you need oil.'

When she didn't or rather couldn't move, Aleksi did, his hands removing hers from the sarong. His mouth, warm now, kissed her shoulder as he parted the sarong and then dropped it.

'Lie down.'

She could feel his breath on her shoulder, could feel the sweat trickling between her breasts, feel his hand on her stomach, and she wanted to weep in shame. But that would only shame her more, so instead she lay there.

Always her body had captured his attention.

He poured oil into his hand before he looked properly at her, and he saw that his hand was shaking a fraction. Those breasts he had once caressed naked were behind fabric and he wanted them exposed. But he wouldn't do that to her here, with paparazzi watching, so he oiled her shoulders and resisted the urge.

He loved her breasts. They were completely natural, without any telling scars beneath the areolaes. He slipped his hand up underneath her armpits, also knowing there were no scars there either. It was a little game he played, and usually his hand met the hard ridge of an implant, but there were no hard edges to Kate; she was soft, unlike him, and she was nervous but she didn't need to be. He saw her frantically try to hold in her stomach, but despite her best efforts when his warm palm met her skin there it was soft rather than taut. Her body was nothing like the many others he had been with, which had all been the same.

Finally, after all these long days and lonely nights, she let him touch her, and it wasn't just her body but her mind that remembered the bliss, and he felt her surrender, felt her accept what she had been resisting, and only then did he lead her inside.

'You're going to hurt me.' There—she'd said it. She stood in his bedroom by his bed and she wanted him so badly. Yet she still wanted to run, because there was no simple solution for her. 'No matter what I do—I know this is going to end up in hurt.'

'I'm not hurting you now.' And he wasn't. 'Just don't fall in love with me, Kate.' Between sentences he kissed her. 'Because only then can I hurt you.' It should have sounded like a threat or a warning, but instead it was more of plea. 'Don't think even for a moment that it can be like this for ever...'

'I don't.' Kate swallowed. She just hoped it instead.

'This is now,' Aleksi said, and slid his hands around her waist. He spoke into her mouth. 'The words I say, the words we say as lovers, don't belong in the future.'

'I don't understand,' she murmured.

'When I say you are beautiful...' His mouth grazed her neck, and then one hand dealt with her bikini. Her breasts tightened briefly at the rush of fanned air, then softened to his warm tongue. 'When I say I want you... That I need you...'

'You actually mean that you won't in the future, right?' She pushed him away furiously. 'Are those words you say so you can close your eyes and go through the motions?'

'Hell! What did he do to you?' Aleksi demanded. 'What did that louse do that you can doubt yourself so much?'

'He *hurt* me, Aleksi, as you're promising you're about to.'

'Only if you think that it can last,' he reiterated. 'Because we both know it can't.'

It couldn't—how could he tell her that soon it might all be gone? That the luxury that bathed her now might soon be over? That even with his bravado, *Krasavitsa* might no longer be his? Oh, he would rise again, would come back from nothing, of that he had no doubt—but he would have to do it alone. Which was why it was imperative she took care of herself. But how could she want him anyway if she knew the truth?

He was back down at her breasts now, buried in them, wanting to get lost in them, but some things had to be said. 'Cash that cheque,' he ordered.

She slapped him in absolute fury. How dared he kiss her breast and at the same time remind her that he was paying her?

'That's what stopping you?' Aleksi would not be thwarted. 'Is that what is stopping you cashing it? Thinking I'm paying you for sex?' Her tears were her answer. 'Then I'll do it for you.' He had never been so hard, had never wanted a woman more, but it had to be business that drove them—this was *his* life that was crashing and burning, not hers, and he couldn't afford to let her glimpse the darkest part of it all.

He left her naked, apart from her bikini bottoms, while he tapped into his computer, and she stood there sobbing with humiliation and shame as he erased all her problems and created a whole set of new ones.

'There…it's done.'

'So now you can have sex with me?' she flung at him.

'Now,' Aleksi said firmly, 'we can forget about it for a while—forget why you are here.'

But she fought with him, avoiding the mouth that was searching for hers. He wanted to resume, to carry on where they'd left off. He had just paid her more money in a moment that she had earned in her entire life and now he expected to sleep with her!

'I have paid for your time, for the façade, for you to hold my hand and kiss me in public. I have paid you for the invasion to your privacy and for your exclusive company over these next weeks.' He pushed her onto the bed and pulled at her bikini while her hand strove to stop his. 'And now it is about choice,' Aleksi insisted when she was naked beneath him. 'Because the money is out of the way now—it is gone, it is done and forgotten. What happens now is your choice.'

But he gave her no choice at all, because her body wept for him...

He was out of his shorts and kissing her hard when suddenly he stopped.

'Tell me to stop now and I promise you will never have to say it again.' His erection was there between her closed thighs, his body on top of hers, his words hot breaths in her ear. He kissed her ear till she furled over on the inside. 'Apart from a kiss in the street, or a handhold on the way to an event...' he was breathing so hard in her ear now she turned her head away '...I will never lay a finger on you again.'

And then he kissed her neck, but still he spoke.

'I don't pay for sex, Kate, and I never have done—you either want me or you don't.'

Her thighs parted a fraction when her lips couldn't, and it was like opening a door a little way and the cat shooting out—except Aleksi didn't quite let himself in.

'It's your choice,' he insisted again, but he was trying to steady himself, because her beckoning warmth was doing strange things to his mind. He found himself wanting to stay just a little longer on the precipice, envisaging the thrill of the jump, but exhilaration was already building, and then he felt her mouth, felt her kiss him, felt her open, and he accepted her warm welcome and crept in.

Not a stab, not a split second, not a dive. Instead, for Kate, there was a slow gathering and filling. He made that moment of entry last for ever. He gathered speed with his thrust, and yet it was like a slow sear deep inside her—slow enough for her to assimilate rapid sensations: him filling her further, the stretch of her body, the moan of relief from him. Then his tongue licked her ear and she felt something new, something close to blind panic, but so much more wonderful than that. All this she felt as Aleksi slid deep inside her.

He beckoned her on his decadent path with a rapid withdrawal, just to the edge, and then he dived in again and again...

And she had never, ever been so intimate with another person before.

Had never been so angry and so desperate and so relieved and so free at the same time, and she told him all that with her body.

She fought—not to get him off, but to pull him deeper and deeper inside her. And harder he went, till she thought she would scream from the pleasure of it, and then she heard that she *was* screaming. It came from another place, this voice that was hers but she'd never before heard.

'I can't.' She heard herself gasp it—then wanted to explain herself, because she wasn't saying she couldn't do it; she was saying she couldn't hold back any longer.

Only words were meaningless now. They were in a different place that spoke a different language, yet Aleksi understood it, because clearly he couldn't hold back either. He was speaking in Russian, and saying her name; he was a different man than she had ever seen or imagined. He was rough and he was tender and he was mindful yet brutal, and so was she—it was another version of Kate that he had exposed. He was so into her, this guarded, sexy, remote man, who was there with her on another level. He made her act like an animal—she was biting and scratching, and her legs were so tight around him that she felt him bucking against her calves. She offered no escape.

Kate was a delicious tourniquet around him, and he shot into her what she craved. They shared the same dizzy high—this rush, this shared sensation that lasted and lasted till she could hear the slowing thud of the bed and realised they were still on the planet, could feel again her body, which she'd surely just climbed out of.

Then she thought about the screams and the bed and the swear-words and the servants—and she did the strangest thing, with him still inside and on top of her. She stared to laugh.

And, strangest of all, Aleksi laughed too.

Then he rolled off and lay beside her and did the unthinkable.

He asked something rather than demanded it of her.

'Will you come to England with me?'

She didn't answer, just turned and looked over to him. He didn't look at her, just stared up at the ceiling, and something told her that her reaction was more important to him than she could even begin to guess.

'Tonight,' Aleksi added, and then he did look over to her. 'Just for a few days—you can bring Georgie, or she can stay with Sophie. Maybe your sister could come and stay here…'

In everything, for more than five years, Georgie had come first with Kate, and of course she still did. But there was actually room in Kate's life now for someone else.

'I'll come,' she said quietly.

'I don't want to unsettle Georgie, but…'

'She'll be fine,' Kate said, because she knew her daughter would be. 'I'll sort that out.'

Then he did something that had never come easily to him.

Kate watched as he nodded his thanks to her and then fell asleep.

Had it been anyone less complex than Aleksi, she'd have thumped him.

CHAPTER NINE

IT WAS freezing in the UK, but Levander and Millie's welcome was warm.

They had a sprawling home on the outskirts of London, and though Kate could see instantly that Aleksi and he were brothers, there was a lightness to Levander, a peace that was missing in Aleksi.

Their house was filled with love and laughter and Kate felt a pang. She wished she'd brought Georgie, but a sixth sense had told her that her daughter would be better off at *home*. Her mother had actually come down from the country for a few days to watch her, and there was Sophie, and her friends, and a party that Georgie felt was too important to miss.

It was her first break from motherhood in almost five years, and it was a guilty relief.

She and Aleksi pretended to be tired when they landed, and were in bed before seven—but it wasn't for sleeping. In the morning, having spoken to Georgie, even though she sounded just fine, Kate found she had to resist constantly phoning to ensure that everything was okay.

'It's like trying not to go back and check if you've put the handbrake on in the car.' Kate described it to Millie. 'Even though you *know* you have...'

'I know.' Millie nodded. 'We left Sashar here when we went to Russia for Dimitri—everyone said that we needed some one-on-one time with him and that it would be better for Sashar too. Especially as Dimitri can be…' she hesitated to summon the right word '…difficult.'

He was certainly that.

Dimitri didn't say a word, didn't join in, and he didn't even seem to be taking an interest in what was going on.

'He does sometimes,' Millie said hopefully. 'He laughed at something Levander said the other day, and he has played a little with Sashar.'

'That's good,' Kate said, and Millie nodded.

'My brother's severely autistic, so I know that Dmitri is interacting a bit—we've just got to be patient.'

Which wasn't a Kolovsky virtue.

Belenki had again dodged all Aleksi's attempts to contact him.

An emergency had arisen, his PA had informed Aleksi.

'He can't help that,' Kate attempted one morning as they sat around a vast indoor pool—it was freezing outside, all the windows were steamed up, but inside the temperature was soaring—and not only due to the luxurious surrounds. Craig was texting constantly now, and she had finally agreed to meet him when she returned, just to get him to leave her alone, which had her on edge. And Aleksi was proving impossible. 'You can't plan for emer…' Her voice trailed off as Aleksi peeled off a page from the newspaper he was reading and there was his nemesis, skiing down a black run in Switzerland.

'That photo's for me,' Aleksi said.

'Don't be ridiculous.' Kate laughed. 'He'll be mortified he's been caught out.' Still she smiled. 'Aleksi, you do it all the time—it's just business.'

'No.' Aleksi shook his head. 'It isn't.'

'Then what?' She didn't get it—she truly didn't get what it was about Belenki that galled him so. 'What is it with him?' she demanded, because she really had to know—his answer, however, just confused her.

'That,' Aleksi said tartly, 'is what I'm trying my damnedest to work out.'

Their *words* thankfully went unnoticed by their hosts, but Kate was sick of his moods, sad that a lovely morning could be ruined by a photo in the newspaper of a man he barely knew—and she told him so, then flounced off to find a better mood in the water.

Levander was playing with Sashar in the pool, and Millie was sitting with Dimitri—who sat where he had been put, his legs dangling in the water, so sheltered and closed, such a contrast to the laughter and boisterousness and sheer joy that came from his little brother.

'Come on, Sashar, jump!' Levander grinned to his son, who had climbed out of the pool and was standing on the edge, nervous but excited as his father urged him on. *'Jump!'*

It took only two tries and then little Sashar stretched out his arms and flew to his father, who caught him. It went on, over and over again, and the squeals of delight made everyone laugh.

Everyone except Dimitri and, Kate realised, Aleksi.

He had been on his phone, replying to an e-mail—only now the e-mail was forgotten. Kate could feel his tension lift, feel the shift as Aleksi looked towards where his brother stood with arms outstretched to Dimitri, whose pale body was shaking as he contemplated taking that brave step.

'How about you, Dimitri?' Levander said in English, and then he repeated it in Russian. 'Jump,' Levander urged. 'I will catch you. I promise.'

But Dimitri just sat there, his eyes looking down.

Levander said it again. '*Preeguy* Dimitri, jump. *Yar tibyar piemaryou*.' And then Aleksi, who wasn't a father, who hadn't been through anything that Levander had, who had no bond with the child, spoke for his nephew.

'Leave him be, Levander.'

Distracted by the warning in his brother's tone, Levander briefly turned around.

'We're just playing. He'll do it when he is ready…' Then he turned his attention back to his new son. 'How about it, Dimitri?'

He spoke again in Russian, but now Kate understood what was being said. What she didn't understand was the tension in Aleksi, who sat beside her like a coiled spring. It was as if he might pounce at any time. Kate glanced over to Millie, who had also picked up on the strange atmosphere.

'Levander is just letting him know that when he is ready to join in…'

'That is not a game.' Aleksi's voice was hoarse. 'It will not help him. Levander!' Aleksi's voice was restrained, but urgent. 'Leave him.'

'Don't tell me how to raise my son.' Levander was less than impressed with his brother's interference.

'They've been playing for ages,' Millie said patiently. 'Levander is not pushing him. Dimitri will go in when he's ready.'

There was something Kate was missing here. Her eyes darted from Aleksi to Sashar who, jealous from lack of attention and wanting some of the fun, climbed out of the pool and ran around the side, laughing and sailing into the air. Then her eyes moved back to Aleksi, whose face was chalk-white. She could see the vein pulsing in his neck as Levander caught his son, and there was fear, real fear in his eyes, as Dimitri stood at the very wrong moment and decided to jump.

'Levander!' Aleksi called to his brother—only Levander didn't need his brother's warning.

He was watching not just Sashar but Dimitri too. He didn't launch himself, it was more a step really, and despite having just caught Sashar, Levander caught Dimitri in time, pulled him into his arms and didn't make too much of a fuss—just held him and encouraged him till Dimitri found his feet on the bottom of the pool.

The steam from the water was rising, a contrast to the icy rain slicing against the windows, and Millie climbed in and took over as Levander glared over to his brother and got out.

'Did you think I would drop him? Did you really think I would deliberately drop him for *fun*?' Levander challenged.

'To show him,' Aleksi corrected. 'To teach him.'

'I know what I'm doing,' Levander snapped. 'I know what he's been through. What sort of a sick person do you think I am? Don't tell me how to raise my son.'

'Would *you*?' Aleksi challenged his older brother. 'When you came to our family, had our father told you to jump would you have done?'

'No,' Levander admitted. 'But I am not Ivan. Dimitri can trust me.'

'Trust no one,' Aleksi sneered. 'That is what Dimitri has been taught.'

'What were *you* taught, Aleksi?' Levander asked, and he didn't sound angry any more.

'To jump,' Aleksi said. 'I stood on the dresser at the bottom of the stairs and he held out his arms and told me to jump. I didn't want to, but he told me to trust him...'

Kate felt sick. She had heard of the ritual, a strange reversal of today's events, where bonding camps made you jump from great heights into the waiting arms of strangers. A ritual that had once been passed from father to son—to toughen them up, to show them the harsh ways of the world.

'So you jumped?' Kate asked in a croak when Levander said nothing. 'And then what?'

'He let me fall,' Aleksi muttered. 'He let me fall and then he picked me up off the floor and held me as I cried. He told me I had been foolish, that I hadn't listened to what he'd told me before—*"nyekamoo doveerye"*—that I should trust no one.'

'He was wrong—' Levander started, only Aleksi didn't want to debate it.

'I'm going to rest.'

For the first time he really limped as he walked off. For the first time he wasn't being proud, or perhaps he didn't have the mental energy to push through the pain. Kate just sat, wondering if she should follow. She guessed he would rather be alone, yet she ached to go after him.

'Sometimes,' Levander said, as the pool door closed on his brother, 'I wonder if the sympathy of my family is misguided. As hellish as my childhood was in the orphanage, I think I might have got off lightly.'

'He was wrong.' It was all Kate could say at first, her mind still whirring with conflict. Because the thought of destroying a child's trust was abhorrent to her, yet things had been different then. 'It was the way men toughened up their children then.'

'Leave it.'

'I don't want to leave it,' Kate answered. 'I'm trying to understand you.'

'Why?'

'Because I…' She hurriedly choked back the word he hated so. 'I care about you.'

'I pay you to care,' Aleksi said coldly.

'Please don't!' she begged. 'Because you know there are some things that can't be bought…'

'I disagree.'

'Well, you're wrong!' Kate sobbed. 'Because—'

"Kate.' Only then did his eyes meet hers, and he might as well have been looking at the wall for all the feeling in them. They were as grey and cold and as impermeable as steel. 'I am not interested in a relationship—I am not interested in your caring. How much more clearly can I say it? All I want now is my business—not just Krasavitsa; I want the lot. And then—' he nodded as he made his mind up '—I want my mother out!'

'How can you speak of her like that?'

'I don't care for her,' Aleksi said. 'I care only for the Kolovsky Empire.'

'You're so cold,' Kate whispered.

'More than cold,' Aleksi said. 'You want to know why I hate her? You want to know why this is nothing but business for me?'

She had wanted to know, but suddenly she was scared. Only there was no stopping Aleksi now.

'I want to understand you,' she told him.

'You couldn't,' Aleksi retorted.

'Maybe if you just let me know you, I will,' she retorted.

'When I was seven, and Christmas was close, my mother said there would be no gifts that year—that I had been too naughty. I knew she must be lying, so I searched for them. She hadn't been lying about that—there were no gifts—and instead I found out their real lie.'

'About Levander?' Kate asked, her stomach tightening as she thought of a seven-year-old boy finding out the family secret. 'I thought they only found out about him being in the orphanage after they came to Australia...'

'They knew,' Aleksi said. 'They knew all along that they had children in the orphanages—but they were too busy living their new lives to care.'

'*Children?*' she gasped.

'Levander is my father's son,' Aleksi said. 'Ivan had a brief fling with his cleaner before he was engaged to my mother. Levander's mother, when she found out she was dying, begged them to take Levander with them to Australia—she had guessed they would soon flee Russia.'

'And you found this out?'

'I found letters,' Aleksi said, 'and certificates. I confronted him...'

Kate knew some of this. She had worked at Kolovsky long enough, had heard the whispers and read the papers, so it came as no real surprise that Ivan and Nina had actually known about Levander all along—but Aleksi hadn't finished yet.

'I found out, too, that there was another child—that before Levander my parents had had a son together.' Beneath his tan his face was grey. 'Not even my brothers know that. I confronted my father with it.'

'And what did he say?'

'He answered me with his fist,' Aleksi said, 'and with

his boots, and with his belt. What scared me…' briefly his eyes met hers '…was not the pain, but his fear.'

She didn't get it. She wanted to ask, to probe, yet she knew to stay silent, and tried so hard not to cry as she heard how badly he had been beaten.

'He was scared and angry and I knew he had no control. That his fear was bigger than him in that moment…' His eyes held hers, awaited her response, and yet she didn't understand, no matter how she wanted to.

'I consoled myself that in that moment his fear overrode his love for me.'

She swallowed. She would go over and over his words later, to try and make sense of them, but for now all she wanted was for him to speak. Only Aleksi was done. Turning his back on her, he stared out of the window. It was so warm inside, so light and airy, it was strange to think that on the other side of the glass it was cold and damp and frozen. She knew she had to reach him, to speak, or he would be gone.

'Nothing overrides love,' she said at last.

'Wrong answer.'

She felt her blood run cold—knew somehow that she had just failed him.

'When you are seven—when you lie on the floor and the man you love, the man you admire, the man you one day want to become beats you, kicks you… When you can see his eyes bulge and feel his spit on your face…'

Her tears were silent, but they were there, flowing down her face as she listened to him.

'You tell yourself this is not your father's doing— that he loves you—that it is the fear that makes him do this…'

'Aleksi—'

'Leave it,' he said. 'I have.'

'How can you?' Kate begged. 'You have another brother. Did you look for him?'

He just stood there.

'Have you found him?'

'No.'

And then she asked the question he dreaded giving an answer to. 'You haven't even *tried* to find him?'

He had never known shame like it—could see the struggle in her eyes as she tried to fathom what even Aleksi couldn't. 'No.'

She really didn't know what to say, so he said it for her.

'I live as my parents have done—a life of greed and debauchery. No, I haven't even tried to find him. So you see, Kate, perhaps it is better that you don't know me, or try to understand me.'

'How could you not—?'

'We should pack,' Aleksi interrupted, the conversation clearly over.

'We should stay,' Kate tried to halt him. 'Maybe if you spoke with Levander, spent some time—'

'I'm done with family,' Aleksi said, and then again he surprised her. 'Thank you.'

'For what?' she asked.

'For making me see...' He gave a small shrug. 'It doesn't matter now.'

As she put her hand up to him he dusted it off and walked out the room, and Kate knew he was also done with her.

Knew then that she shouldn't have spoken, should only have listened, because her response *had* been wrong.

As right and logical as it had seemed to her, as she

replayed his words she let her tears fall as she realised what she had just done.

If, as she'd stated, nothing overrode love, then to Aleksi it must be simple—she'd just taken from him the last semblance of his father's love.

CHAPTER TEN

'THERE'S a job going in Bali...'

Kate walked along the beach and tried to take in what Craig was telling her. 'Well, not a job as such, but I've got friends there, and the surfing is good. I've been wanting to go for ages.'

'But you didn't?'

'I wanted to know you were okay—I know I'm not a good dad, but I just...' he pulled his hand through his long blond hair. 'Now you're okay, now that you and Georgie are going to be looked after...'

'You feel that you can?'

'I'll write to her. I'll send her cards, and I'll save up so she can come for a holiday. My parents are hoping to bring her out for a couple of weeks. Here...' He wasn't after money; he was here to give it. 'I know I can remember birthdays, but for Easter, for when she gets a good school report...'

She stood there as he gave her everything he could afford for his daughter—just not his time.

'We want different things for her, Kate. I want waves and freedom, and you want schools and routines...'

'*She* wants schools and routines,' Kate said, but she wasn't arguing with him. She actually got it—he certainly wouldn't make father of the year, but in his own way he did love Georgie, and Kate would always tell her that.

'Will you let my parents bring her out to see me?' he asked.

'Of course I will,' Kate said, and even if it wasn't much, somehow she was touched, because he had at least stayed around to make sure they would be okay before he left.

He just didn't know it was all a lie.

'I've got good taste in louses,' Kate tried to joke, and she cried a little inside for herself and for Georgie.

She wished Craig well, hugged him and gave him a brief kiss, and as she walked back to the house she surprised herself—because she actually felt free.

Aleksi was having a revelation all of his own.

'Have it.'

Monday morning at nine, he had stepped off the plane and headed straight to the office. He'd been ready to fight his mother for everything, and now Nina had handed it to him on a plate.

'I can't fight you any more, Aleksi…'

He stood unmoved by Nina's tears.

'Have Kolovsky, have Krasavitsa—just please hear Belenki out. Maybe I am wrong, maybe I have been greedy, but some of his ideas are good…'

He didn't get her.

If he lived to be a thousand he would never get her. Always he would hate her, but sometimes, bizarrely, he wondered if he could summon love for her too.

'You've changed your mind.' He was tired of this—so damn tired of this. 'Why?'

'Sheikh Amallah cancelled the Princess's order, and others have cancelled too. Lavinia has told me she is leaving—that I can stick my job and she'll only work for you…'

Aleksi glanced over to where Lavinia stood and gave her a thin smile of welcome as the rebel returned from the coup. Then he dismissed her as Nina carried on shredding tissues.

'Others have too—and then I saw the samples of Kolovsky bedlinen for the supermarket chain and I knew I had sold out. I know I am a poor businesswoman. No matter how I enjoy it, I see that everything your father built I am ruining…'

'Then stop,' Aleksi said simply, because he could not make himself embrace or comfort her.

'I *am* stopping. I will concentrate on the charities. But please,' Nina begged, 'hear Belenki out.'

'I can't get hold of Belenki,' Aleksi said wearily.

'He's here,' Nina said, and Aleksi's blood ran cold. 'Rather, he arrives this morning; I am supposed to be meeting with him at two. Please talk with him, Aleksi. Always he confuses me—he is so strong, so forceful— and always I end up agreeing with what he suggests, always he tells me I am helping the orphans…'

It was guilt that drove her. Aleksi could almost see it.

He drove along the beach road back home and the adrenaline was still coursing in his veins—because he had expected a fight with his mother and then got tears and capitulation. Guilt for what she had done in abandoning her son and a stepson to awful childhoods in Russian orphanages. She tried to purge it by raising millions for charity.

He just didn't know if he had enough left of his soul to forgive himself, let alone Nina, for not trying to right her sins long ago.

Didn't know if he could ever find peace—and then he turned the key in his door and almost glimpsed it.

Walking into his house, Aleksi saw the dust of sand on the tiles, Georgie's boogie board discarded, and the apologetic expression of his housekeeper.

'I'm sorry, I haven't got around...'

'It's not a problem,' Aleksi said, and he meant it. 'Leave it—take the day off,' he offered, because he needed to be alone.

Since Kate and Georgie had moved in every homecoming was different he realised. Everything was different—even his fridge contents, Aleksi thought as he pulled it open.

Oh, there were still exotic fruit juices and imported beers, still fancy cheeses, but there were also juice boxes and little animal shaped processed cheeses that tasted disgusting but were strangely addictive.

He was growing used to waking up to laughter and conversation and chaos—chaos because even with a nanny and a housekeeper and the most efficient team of staff, every morning without fail Georgie lost something. Every morning there was a mad dash for the front door.

But not for much longer.

He didn't need Kate now.

Except maybe he did.

He walked upstairs to the neatly made bed and saw her book on the bedside, picked it up and checked the page.

She was at 342 and it had been 210 on the plane.

So, she had been reading it when he'd thought she was sulking—why did that make him smile?

She had tried to talk to him since his revelation, had

told him that she would try to understand, that maybe it wasn't too late to look for his brother.

Could he do it?

Could he let her in? Could he trust not her but himself?

Not just with her future, but with Georgie's?

Could she even want a man who had chosen to turn his back on his brother?

It wasn't just monogamy that Kate wanted, but his truth, his thoughts, his soul. It was a lot to consider giving, and yet… He put down the book, smelt her perfume in the room and realised he had a lot to lose, too.

More than he could stand.

He would tell her—tell her what he didn't know. About this fear that woke him at night, about the answer he was so close to remembering, about the shame that filled him each time he thought of Riminic, the brother he had left behind all these years.

How could he ask Kate to have faith in him when he didn't know his own truth?

He walked across the bedroom, stared out at the bay—a view he had seen maybe a million times but he'd never really looked at before. All it was was a backdrop, a view he paid for, to impress but not to enjoy—but he did so now. The water was so smooth there was barely a ripple, shades of grey with steaks of azure, and then if you looked deeper there was aqua and silver and brown. It mocked Kolovsky silk over and over, because nothing could be as powerful and beautiful as nature.

The bay changed—not each day, not even each minute, but with every shift of focus, every look, there was more to see.

So, so much more to see.

Nyekamoo doveerye.

His father had been dead for two years, but as sure as if he was standing beside him Aleksi heard Ivan's voice—and, to his regret, Aleksi conceded that his father was right.

She was walking. A sheer white sarong covered her, but not enough. Even from this distance he could see the curves barely leashed by a bikini.

Money did suit her, Aleksi thought darkly.

Those wild curls were sleeker and glossier now, and her skin glowed. He could see the flash of her jewellery and the golden dust of her tan, and she had a new-found confidence that he'd been stupid enough to think he might have given her.

"Nyekamoo doveerye"—trust no one.

The man was as blond as Georgie, and Aleksi just knew that it was Craig who was walking in step beside Kate now.

They were together.

There was an ease to them that sliced at his heart.

There was a togetherness that unleashed his anger like a snarling dog let loose.

Disgust churned black and bilious in his stomach.

Foolishness mocked him too, for daring to believe for a little while that she might be different—that he could be too.

But as Craig kissed her, as he pulled her into his arms and she leant on him for a moment, it wasn't jealousy that ate Aleksi alive—that would come ten seconds later—it was regret.

Regret that it wasn't him.

That Georgie wasn't his.

That there could be no *them* after all.

* * *

'Hey!' There was an elation to her as she stepped into his home that he might once have been foolish to think had been caused by him. 'What are you doing back?'

His muscles were shot with adrenaline, the hairs on his neck stood up, and he was slightly breathless. His body was screaming for him to fight, to confront, but he just stood there waiting, needing to hear her lie, and somehow, still at the eleventh hour, hoping she wouldn't.

'Where were you?'

'Just walking.' Kate smiled, because jet lag didn't factor when you'd snuggled in gold pyjamas reading, eating and dozing all the way from England. 'It's a gorgeous day. What are you doing home?'

'I came for my computer,' Aleksi said. 'The real one.'

'The one you've been hiding from Nina!" Kate laughed, and the sound of it made him sick. 'Why?'

'Belenki is here.' He glanced at her skin, at the dust of sand on her legs, and then to her face, to the lips that smiled at him but had just been kissed by another man. 'Get dressed,' he said. 'We meet him at my office in an hour.'

She didn't want to get dressed.

Aleksi was right—she was on a high. There was a dizzy elation to her that she had never expected to come today.

There was freedom, there was lust, and there was still the prickly warmth from the sun on her shoulders and the salty smell of the bay in her nostrils. And before her was Aleksi.

She could feel his tension, knew it must be because he was meeting Belenki, and as she had done once before she wanted to soothe him.

Wanted *him*.

Whatever his past, she wanted his future—so badly. He made her bold, he made her ache with want, and although she felt his bristling anger she wanted to soothe him, so she stepped towards him.

'It's only a thirty-minute drive,' she murmured.

She pressed into him, smelt not the ocean but him, felt his hands on her arms and placed her lips on his.

And he thought about it. Feeling her hot and oiled beneath his fingers, he thought about it. So angry, he was hard; so beguiled, he wanted release. He could feel her tongue roll around his, urging a response, and although he knew where those lips had just been he let her kiss on.

He hadn't cried in decades—not even when beaten. The last time he had wept was when he had lain on the floor and his father had warned him to trust no one, and yet now there was a sting in his eyes and such tension in his lips that he couldn't kiss her back. He just felt the roll of her tongue.

God, but she had a nerve!

Her sarong was off—was it her fingers or his that had done it?—and the top of her bikini was gone. Her breasts splayed against his chest, her heat pressed into him and his fingers dug into her generous buttocks.

She was grappling with his belt, but he would not give her an inch.

He pulled her so tight into him that she gasped.

Her mouth was on his cheek and his burning anger impaled her. He dug his fingers in deeper to her flesh, and he was so turned on he wanted to forget what he had seen. He wanted her so badly that it actually hurt to resist.

He wanted her seduction, yet he craved survival more. But still he let her.

He let her kiss him, let his body respond to her, just enough to inflame them both.

He could feel the hum of her lips on his neck, feel her frantic search for his skin, her hand tearing at his shirt, and then the nibble of her teeth on his neck. He slipped his fingers into her bikini bottoms, felt the heat of her intimate skin and like an addict he craved just once more. But Aleksi was stronger than that—he was a man who could come off pain medication in one night; he could surely withdraw more easily from her, couldn't he?

Yet she was more addictive.

Her hand was at his zipper, and it was a more skilled hand now, because she freed him in seconds.

He wanted her bikini off, but there wasn't even time for that, so he parted the material with his erection and entered her, feeling the scrape of her bikini along his length as he pushed into her. He could sense the throb of her orgasm around him, felt her sob and moan as she convulsed around his length, and he was a second away from joining her.

Yet he was stronger than that. As she ground into him, demanded his response, screamed his name, the triumph was his as he pulled back, still erect, unsated—and, she now registered, loaded with contempt.

'Aleksi?'

She had never been so naked, so exposed, so confused, tumbling down from the throes of orgasm to see his look of pure loathing.

'I told you.' He pulled up his zipper and crucified her with his eyes. 'Get dressed.'

For Kate, it was the ultimate in rejection.

This logical voice inside her mind told her he was

tired, stressed, late for the meeting, yet her gut told her otherwise.

She sat beside him as he drove in silence, her mind going over and over what had taken place, trying and failing to remember his response—she had been so deeply into him, so confident, so sure, so *open* with him, his fleeting resistance hadn't confused her at the time.

It confused her now.

She could still feel the imprint of his fingers in her buttocks, and as she stared out of the window at the bay that stayed still as they hurtled towards the city, she could recall his initial imperviousness to her kisses—only she had won him round. No, she'd *thought* she had won him round.

She just wasn't used to these grown-up games.

Her seduction had been her own, her devotion absolute. There had been nothing else on her mind other than him. Her motives had perhaps not been virtuous, but they had been pure—she had only wanted to make love with him.

The bay view had gone now. There was no view from her window other than shops and cafés and people and trams and cars. It was too busy for her cluttered mind to cope with so she turned to him, yet there was nothing there.

Just this dark brooding stranger with a mind she could never begin to fathom.

They pulled in outside the office. The doorman jumped, the valet parker was already moving. Aleksi was keen to get to Belenki—but Kate just sat there.

'What happened back there, Aleksi?' she asked quietly.

'What?' He frowned, as if he had no idea what she was talking about.

'What *happened*?' She could hear her voice rising to a feminine, needy pitch and fought to check it, fought to check herself, to reel herself back, to heed his earlier warning—that love, a future, was something he would never be prepared to give her.

'I changed my mind.' A cruel smile twisted his lips. 'Which is a man's prerogative.'

Slap.

Her hand sliced the air, struck at his cheek. He made no move to halt it. Worse, he gave no reaction to it, and she watched as the doorman discreetly closed the door and backed away, watched the smoothness of his cheek turn red, saw the shape of her fingers on his flesh. It didn't even move him.

'I trusted you.' He said nothing as she voiced her truth. 'I could accept that it wasn't for ever, I agreed to your rules, to your twisted logic. But in bed, with us, when we made love, I trusted you.' She saw him blink. It was his only reaction, but it was more than she'd come to expect and so she told him—told him exactly what he had just done to her. 'Even when you whispered that you would always want me—' she saw him blink again '—I stuck to the rules and told myself it was passion talking. But I didn't deserve that.' He closed his eyes for a second, but she would not let him shut her out. 'I trusted you with my body, Aleksi. I felt safe and gorgeous and free of shame. When we made love I thought in that, at least, we were on the same level—that whatever else we had, that was something honest between us.'

'Did you feel safe and gorgeous and free of shame when you were on the beach with *Craig*?' Livid eyes turned to her, because he wanted to see this—wanted her eyes to widen when she realised that he knew, wanted to watch her fall from the dizzy heights of her moral high ground and scrabble on the floor to pick herself up with fractured reasons and excuses.

'Actually, yes,' Kate said simply, and she opened her own door and stepped out. 'We've got a meeting to go to.'

'You were unfaithful to me,' Aleksi sneered.

'No.' She walked to the lift with her head held high—walked just a step in front of him and only spoke again when the lift doors were safely closed behind them. 'I finally felt free because Craig was telling me he was moving overseas. I finally felt free because he wasn't asking for money and he wasn't suddenly deciding he wanted to take Georgie with him. I felt free because finally we'd worked out our boundaries. You could have spoken to me, Aleksi. You could have asked what I was doing with him, asked me to explain what was going on, instead of screwing the truth out of me.'

He gave a black laugh. 'What, and give you a chance to come up with excuses?'

'I don't need your chances, Aleksi, and I don't need your mistrust.' She had never felt so weak, so floored, so raw, and yet somehow she had never felt so strong as she walked into her old office and stood at her old desk. 'And I don't need to make excuses.' She fixed him with a stare and she meant every word that she said. 'We're done.'

'So why are you still here?' Aleksi demanded.

'Because, unlike you, I have a moral compass. I have a daughter too, and the cleaner the break the less the impact on her. If you don't mind, I'd like to tell Georgie back at the house, and then we'll find a hotel.'

'Kate…'

'I don't want to hear it, Aleksi.'

'Tell me exactly what you were doing with him and maybe then...'

'You'll forgive me? Or will it suddenly be acceptable to you? I'll prove that this time you were mistaken? But what about next time, Aleksi? What happens next time you decide I'm not trustworthy?' She shook her head, and she was so angry she wanted to hit him again—only this time she stopped herself. The tears that were building inside her she would save for later. 'What you did to me back there,' Kate said, 'I'll never understand and I'll never forgive. But I'm not going to be a martyr and give you back your money—after what you just did to me I've earned every last cent of your million dollars. In fact, *you* owe *me*!'

What she was saying should have killed him, should have hurt, should have shamed him—except he was beyond all that. He was numb, frozen, locked up—because in their darkest moment he wasn't even thinking about her.

Coming towards him was a walking nightmare—one he'd never been able to wake from. One he'd never been able to adequately describe or recall, except in the black moths that fluttered and taunted his shattered memory as logic tried to pin them down. They all gathered now, as clear as day, and walked right up to him.

'Aleksi,' Zakahr Belenki announced as he stood before him. 'I believe we have much to discuss.'

CHAPTER ELEVEN

'STAY.'

Rarely did Kate sit in on meetings—and especially not since she had been masquerading as his fiancée.

His *ex*-fake fiancée she reminded herself. But stay she did, because Aleksi's face was suddenly grey.

The air was thick with tension and Kate didn't really understand why. Sure, Zakahr Belenki was a difficult customer—he had his claws in Kolovsky, thanks to Nina, and it would be hard extricating them—but Aleksi was more than up to the task.

'We seem to keep missing each other.' Zakahr's Russian accent was pronounced.

He shook Aleksi's hand and nodded to Kate, but she could feel the animosity sizzling between them and suddenly all she wanted was out.

There was danger here. She could smell it.

Despite the designer suits and opulent surroundings there was something primitive about them—two gang lords meeting. Despite the white smiles, their eyes were black as they locked.

'I don't think so.' Aleksi dismissed the polite observation. 'I have made every effort to meet. You, Zakahr, have been the one who has been unavailable.'

'Well, I'm here now.' Zakahr gave a brief shrug. 'Where is Nina?'

'*I* am head of Kolovsky,' Aleksi said. 'You speak with *me*.'

'Of course,' Zakahr replied. 'As you know, I have an exciting vision for the House of Kolovsky,' Zakahr went on, 'and it will benefit my charity with a percentage—'

Aleksi put up his hand to stop him. 'You are a brilliant businessman,' Aleksi said. 'As am I. You must know that this is only a short-term gain—that in two years the exclusive name we have built will be no more.'

'My priority is to my charity. Nina assures me—'

'Nina speaks rubbish,' Aleksi interjected. 'If Nina had her way you could buy Kolovsky toilet paper in the two-dollar shop—where,' he added, '*we* would all be working. Don't hide behind your charity in *this* office.'

'Okay.'

There was a mirthless smile on the edge of Zakahr's lips, and it made Kate uncomfortable. It was the winning edge she had seen in Aleksi when he held a full hand, and suddenly she was scared—of what, Kate didn't know, but she was scared all the same.

'Kolovsky is raising millions for your charity,' Aleksi pointed out. 'That stream will continue for as long as Kolovsky is strong—yet this plan you propose to my mother, while it might bring you an initial surge of income, will rapidly end. Kolovsky will dry like a stream in the desert if we follow this through—you and I both know it. Your aim is to crush Kolovsky.'

Kate felt her breath hold in her lungs as Aleksi threw down the most outlandish suggestion. But then he reiterated it.

'You *want* the business to go under.'

'Why would I want that?' Zakahr frowned. 'I am serious about my charity.'

'Don't play your games with me,' Aleksi said coldly. 'The truth, or leave!'

'You really want the truth?'

'Oh, I want it,' Aleksi gritted out. 'I want to hear how you plan to crush Kolovsky—how in two years you hope to—'

'Aleksi...' As his PA, Kate would never have dared interrupt, even as his make-believe fiancée she had no right to, but his accusations were so outlandish, his anger so palpable, she couldn't contain herself. He was walking into a trap and she wanted to warn him.

It never entered her head that Aleksi already knew it was there...

'You're right,' Zakahr admitted bluntly. 'My hope is that in two years I sit at your desk on my annual visit to Australia. That it will be the House of Belenki which produces the silks that make women weep with greed.'

Kate just sat, her mouth agape.

'Your mother brings me coffee, or perhaps she cleans the stairs when I walk in with my filthy shoes...' He stopped. 'That is the dream—but I will settle for reality. I will accept the House of Kolovsky's complete demise...'

Why?

Kate wanted to ask, but she sat there silent, waiting for Aleksi to demand the same—except he didn't.

'Don't you want to know why?' Zakahr asked finally, when Aleksi said nothing.

'I already know why,' he said quietly.

'You know *nothing*,' Zakahr sneered. 'You sat there drunk at a fundraising ball as I spoke of my childhood, of how I prostituted myself just to survive. You simply snapped your fingers for more champagne, and then the world wept when the next day you wrapped your car around a tree. You write a cheque and your work is done. Iosef at least makes an effort, Levander tries too—even your sister is making amends. But you, Aleksi, have forgotten your roots.'

'Never,' he denied.

'You live a gluttonous, debauched life that is built on shame—'

'There's no shame!' Kate countered, her voice thin and pale in the crackling silence.

Zakahr's face was bleached in hate, as if at any moment he might leap across the desk and take Aleksi's throat in his hands. But worse, and most confusing for Kate, was the fact that Aleksi just sat there, leaning back in his chair, his eyes narrowing as each accusation was hurled. So it was she who jumped in.

'The Kolovskys have already acknowledged what happened to Levander...'

'This isn't about Levander,' Aleksi said, but he didn't look at Kate. His eyes were on Zakahr.

'Your fake boyfriend is right,' Zakahr said. 'I've been through the figures—he's certainly paying you well!' he sneered in her direction. 'This isn't about Levander. This is about revenge.'

'Revenge?' Kate swallowed.

'You want the truth?' Zakahr challenged Aleksi. 'Well, here it is.'

'I told you—I already know the truth.'

Only now did Aleksi look at Kate, and she saw the slate-grey of his eyes. Even as her eyes darted to Zakahr, even before Aleksi spoke again, Kate knew it too—realised a little more of the pain he carried.

'Kate, this is my brother, Zakahr.'

She saw the dart of surprise in Zakahr's eyes, saw him swallow before speaking.

'You know?'

Aleksi nodded.

'For how long?'

'That it was you?' Aleksi asked the question. 'Only now do I know that for sure.' He continued, almost speaking to himself. 'Ivan and Nina had another child. They had a relationship when they were young and broke up for a while—which was when Ivan fathered Levander—you, Zakahr, are my full brother.'

Then he told him about the certificates he had found aged seven, that he had found out his kin were being raised in orphanages.

Riminic Ivan Kolovsky.

Levander Ivan Kolovsky.

There had been no Zakahr.

'I changed my name,' Zakahr explained. 'Not at first. I ran away and worked the street for several years, and you don't need a name there. A charity like the one I run now offered me a way out. It was then—when I was a man, when I had picked myself out of the gutter—that I swore revenge. It was only then—when I wasn't eating out of garbage cans, when I wanted an education—that I needed a name. Perhaps you can see why I chose not to take my father's.' He looked at Aleksi with loathing. 'Did you never think to look for me?'

'I didn't know. I couldn't remember,' Aleksi said.

'You found out when you were seven—you are a man now.'

Kate just sat there—she didn't know what to say, because Zakahr was right. With all Aleksi's means, with all his money, with everything at his disposal, *shouldn't* he have at least looked?

After the longest silence Aleksi spoke. 'I thought I was going mad. I thought I had brain damage from the accident. For months now—all the months since the accident—I have been trying to work it out; I thought the accident had robbed me of my memory,' Aleksi explained, 'though now I see it actually brought things back.'

Zakahr opened his mouth to speak, but as Aleksi continued he stayed silent.

'I knew something was wrong before the accident. I was out of control, but I didn't know why. I hated seeing you at the charity ball, but after you left I tried to speak with you—I was driving to the airport when the accident happened and I didn't even know what for. I didn't know you were my brother.'

'Please!' Zakahr retorted. 'You've just told me that you *knew* you had a brother in an orphanage in Russia, you *knew* you reacted emotionally when you saw me, when you heard about my past, and you expect me to believe that it never entered your head that it might be me?'

'After the accident I could remember the beating my father gave me when I was seven as clear as anything. I could remember finding the certificates, demanding to know about you. You can believe it or not, though I swear this is the truth—until then I had no recall of it, even when Levander arrived...' He looked back on those years with different eyes now. 'It was a shock to find out about him.' Aleksi shook his head as if to clear it, as he struggled to join together the pieces of his mind from before and after that fateful day. 'Only after the accident did I remember what I had found out all that time ago. The revelation all those years before had completely disappeared from my memory.' He shook his head again, but in bemusement. 'How?'

'He literally knocked it out of you,' Zakahr said, and Aleksi just sat there, stunned. 'For a child to survive, sometimes the brain is kind and allows denial. I know because there are things I have done that I don't remember—just sometimes I wake up in the night...'

'And you know you've glimpsed hell?' Aleksi murmured. He knew because he had.

After that restless night at the ball had led him to Kate's door once more he had headed for the airport, filled with a need to put matters right with Zakahr, to face what he was facing now.

'I have thought of revenge for a long time.' Zakahr said. 'It has been my one sure goal—to bring you all down.'

'Have your revenge, then,' Aleksi said. 'There will be no argument from me.'

'You might want to speak with your lawyer first,' Zakahr responded. 'Shore up your assets, close a few doors...' He frowned when Aleksi shook his head. 'But surely you would want to protect the people that you love?'

'Levander, Iosef, myself—we can all take care of ourselves. I have already taken care of the others that matter.'

'I understand,' Zakahr said.

And suddenly so too did Kate, and she saw a drop of salt water land on her lap, replaying so many conversations through tear-filled eyes. She knew now why Aleksi had so badly wanted her to cash the cheque. Somehow, even though he had hurt her today more than she thought she could bear, he had been taking care of her.

'What about Krasavitsa?' Belenki checked. 'Your mother said before you would never step down from that without a fight.'

'Take it,' Aleksi stated emotionlessly. 'If it makes you feel better.'

He had lost everything.

He had lost her.

There was no thrill, no elation, no victory, no peace.

He had nothing to give, nothing to offer to make it up to her.

Aleksi knew that as he drove her to his home for the final time.

His past—his shame, his family's shame—had all finally caught up with them. After his mistrust, his treatment of Kate, he knew, because he had finally let himself know *her*, that there would be no going back for the two of them.

He had hurt her at her very core.

But the old Aleksi suddenly jumped on his shoulder, whispering in his ear as he hugged the bends on the beach road, grinding the gears, accelerating out of bends, trying to justify the way he'd treated her. She had been with her ex, she'd kissed him, he'd seen it…

What had *she* seen? he asked himself.

Over the years, as he'd ricocheted from scandal to scandal, what had the woman who'd loved him throughout it all silently endured?

He looked over to her and knew he was right about how she felt about him—and it wasn't vanity or presumption, as it once had been. Her love had been different, and so rare he hadn't recognised it. A steadfast love that had been there beside him through bad times as well as good, and now, because of his actions, it was lost.

'I'm sorry.'

The old Aleksi would have attempted to lighten the silence that followed his apology, would have confused her with casual words like, *We can finish what we started*, would have made her blink till she wondered if she'd misread what had happened, till he convinced her that she had.

'For what?' she asked.

'All of it.' They were nearing his house and he slowed down to slide through the electric gates. 'Had I known, had I understood that Zakahr was my brother, had I known just how toxic my family's history really was, I would never have exposed you to it. I would never have brought you and Georgie to my home at such a time. I knew something was wrong. I had no idea just how wrong it all was.'

'I don't care about your family's mistakes! All I cared about was you,' she cried.

They were home, or at his house anyway, and she climbed out of the car.

'I am sorry, too, for accusing you about what happened before...'

'For what?' Kate wanted him to say it out loud.

'For what happened,' he repeated.

'For *what*?' she pressed.

'For...' He didn't know how to describe it, but he tried. 'For holding back from you when we last made love.'

She laughed a black laugh as she went into the house—because that was exactly what he had done. 'You hold back in everything, Aleksi. You hold yourself back because you're so damn scared of falling.'

Oh, she would have said more, but the trouble with being a parent was that at times it included children. Little girls who arrived home when they shouldn't. And even though she wanted to scream and shout and kick and fight, Kate knew that instead she had to smile, to swallow down her loss and anger and pretend it didn't hurt, to convince her daughter that leaving was a good idea, that they were better off without him, that Mummy was absolutely and completely fine…

Only tears were so appallingly close, Kate realised with horror, that she couldn't do it right now.

Couldn't be brave at this second.

'Hi, there!' It was Aleksi who filled the crushing silence as Georgie climbed out of the car. 'How was school?'

'I hate it,' Georgie said, and then promptly burst into tears. 'I hate it and I'm never going back!'

Oh, yes, the trouble with being a parent was that even when you had a top-notch nanny children still wanted their mother—even when there wasn't a single bit of you left to give, still they demanded that you produce it.

'What happened?'

They were somehow in the kitchen. Aleksi got a juice box from the fridge and Kate thought Georgie might push it away, but she actually took it and then, when Aleksi left them to it, she gulped it down before speaking.

'I don't like it there,' Georgie sobbed. 'Tell me I don't have to go back.'

'Not till you tell me what happened!' Kate repeated. She knew she wasn't handling this well, knew she should wait for her to open up, but her nerves were so taut they were close to snapping. She wanted it out now and sorted, so she could get on with her own pain. She didn't want Georgie's drama today. Tomorrow, yes, and the next day, and the next too—but not today, when her own heart was bleeding and breaking. Except she was a mother, so she didn't get to choose. 'Talk to me, Georgie.'

'I just don't like it,' she said. 'The other girls are mean.'

'What did they say?' Kate asked, and she could hear the shrill note in her own voice that undid all the good of the cool juice and made Georgie cry just a bit harder.

'Why don't you have a swim?'

It was Aleksi who came in, and even though Kate loathed him, even though she knew she would be far, far better off without him, she was actually relieved when he took over the reins. She was so used to holding them alone it felt different as he steered things a little— perhaps not in the direction she would have, but maybe another route was called for.

'Have a swim, I'll get some snacks brought out, and then when you've cooled down maybe you can tell your mum what's going on.'

'Will you swim too?' Georgie's eyes swung to her mother's.

'Sure,' Kate said, though it was absolutely the last thing she wanted.

'And you?' Georgie's eyes narrowed at Aleksi, and Kate couldn't help but sense a small challenge coming from her daughter. 'Will you swim, too?'

'Of course,' he responded immediately.

Kate took for ever to reluctantly haul on her bikini, although Georgie had changed in less than a second. Aleksi was out there, and she really couldn't face this...

Her face started to crumple as she heard the laughter from her daughter, and she looked out as Aleksi threw a ball and realised what she had to tell the little girl.

That they were moving again. That Aleksi and her

mum's relationship was over. That her dad had gone to
Bali, permanently...

'Catch me!'

Georgie's voice soared through the late-afternoon
sky and Kate's throat tightened on a shout of warning
as she saw Georgie run. Aleksi was turning to get the
ball, too far from the little girl who ran to the edge. She
slipped, soaring through the air, and Kate's heart was in
her mouth as the world moved in slow motion—she was
too close to the edge, and would surely crack her head!
Only Aleksi moved like lightning, stretching though
the water and pulling Georgie back with millimetres to
spare. He caught her. Oh, there was a splash, and they
both went under, and Georgie had a mouth and nose full
of water, but somehow he caught her.

'Never do that again.' Aleksi's voice was close to a
shout, and real fear was on his features by the time Kate
had dashed through the house and out to the pool. 'You
could have had an accident.'

'You caught me, though.'

'I might not have...' Aleksi sat her down at the pool's
edge and Kate could see that beneath his tan he was pale.
'I almost didn't!'

'But you did!' Georgie said simply.

'Georgie...' Kate realised her voice was shaking. 'You
warn people properly. You don't just jump. You slipped
and might have really hurt yourself.'

'He caught me, though,' Georgie insisted, but her face
was working up to tears.

'Leave it,' Aleksi said gruffly. 'You're fine—you're
safe. I'm only upset because...' He was helpless at her
tears. 'Because I care about you.'

'No, Aleksi, you *don't*!' she snarled, and then she
turned and challenged her mother. 'Everyone at school

knows it's just pretend. Lucy's nanny is a friend of Sophie…' She stared accusingly at Kate. 'She heard them talking, and she said that soon he's getting rid of us!'

'Nobody's getting rid of you!' Aleksi's voice was a husk of breath.

'But it is going to end,' Georgie said. 'I could hear you rowing.'

'Grown-ups argue sometimes,' Aleksi explained, still stunned.

'When are we going home?'

Georgie's voice was shrill and Kate felt sick. 'We're getting a new home darling.' She tried to smile, tried to sound positive, tried to make it sound idyllic as she crushed her own daughter's heart. 'Near your new school.'

'So it's true, then?'

Georgie was too proud to crumple there and then, but with a sob she ran up to her bedroom, leaving Kate with the guilt she had always known would come since she'd embarked on this dangerous game—only she had never anticipated how devastating it would be.

'Kate!' Aleksi called her back as she rushed to follow her daughter, but she ignored him, so he barred the door with his body. 'You've done nothing wrong. She'll be okay once you are in your home, once she's really settled in her new school…'

'You don't get it, do you?' Kate choked. 'You think it's about the house and the nice cars and the pool and the posh school…' God, she truly hated him in that moment. 'She doesn't give a stuff about all that. She loved *you*, she loved our little family, she actually believed that you loved us too…'

And not even Aleksi could halt her, so desperate was

she to get to her daughter, so he didn't even try. He stood aside and listened to Kate somehow not pound up the steps but calmly walk, blowing her nose as she did so. Then he heard the gentle knock on Georgie's bedroom door.

Walking had been painful for Aleksi since the accident, but it was sheer agony today as he forced himself, physically forced himself, to take each step. Every instinct told him to turn, to run away, yet he made himself undertake the most daunting walk of his life.

'Why doesn't he love us?'

He heard Georgie's sobs and he could feel the sweat beading on his forehead. He so badly wanted to fling open her door, to counter Kate's words, yet he did what Kate had so rightly accused him of.

He held back.

'Aleksi has a lot going on in his life.' He heard her trying to sound calm and assured. 'Lots of difficult things are happening with his family right now. There are going to be lots of rows and arguments and he doesn't want us to get mixed up in at all...'

'But we could help him,' Georgie begged. 'We could be nice to him when they are all being mean.'

'It's not that simple, darling.'

Aleksi closed his eyes as he listened to Kate attempt to soothe her daughter.

'Aleksi isn't sure what's going to happen with his work with his home...'

'Why can't he live with us in our new home?' Georgie reasoned. 'You said we're getting a nice new home near the school.'

'We are, but...'

'So why can't he live with us there?'

'It's not going to be what Aleksi's used to,' Kate said, and she couldn't gloss it up any more.

Defeated, she sat on the bed where her daughter lay sobbing and stroked her shoulder, tried to comfort her, and wished someone could comfort her too—because all Georgie's arguments had done was ram home the cruel truth. Aleksi didn't want them. Yes, he cared, and had ensured they would be looked after, but their little world wasn't one that was for him. Soon he would be healed, back to his playground world. Aleksi would build himself up again—and it wouldn't be with her.

He had told her that from the start. She had gambled her heart and had thought she knew the odds, that the prize of an education and security for her daughter was worth the risk. But sitting on the bed, realising her future was without the man she loved, thinking of the pain she had caused Georgie, suddenly Kate was angry. The glimpses of his love, the tastes of what he could never sustain—surely it would have been better without that? Better to live not knowing what she was missing?

'I thought he loved us...' Georgie sobbed into her pillow. 'I told all the girls that I had a new daddy....'

Maybe she shouldn't have, Kate thought to herself, but who could blame her? Just as she had played dress-up as a little girl, who could blame Georgie for wanting what so many other children had? Kate wanted to give in then—just wanted to stop being brave and strong and sensible. She wanted to lie down on the bed with her daughter and wail, and bemoan how unfair it all was sometimes, but she wouldn't allow herself. For a second she wavered, felt the swell of tears in her throat, and then she felt his hand on her shoulder, comforting her as she comforted her daughter, and Kate held her breath.

'Georgie...' Aleksi's usually curt voice was soft, but

unwavering. 'Nothing would make me more proud than to be your father.'

'So why are you sending us away?' Her pinched, angry and tired little face swung around to confront him.

Yes, she was tired, Kate realised, and her heart twisted in on itself. The journey that was so hard for her at times was hard on Georgie too. No matter how she tried to shield her, no matter how she tried to protect her, her little girl was tired and confused too.

'I am not sending you away,' Aleksi explained. 'Part of me wants you and your mother to leave because I think it might be easier on you both.'

'How?'

Georgie sat up as Aleksi sat down.

'Your mother told you that things might be difficult if you stay.'

'I don't care about that.'

'I see that now,' Aleksi said. 'Georgie, I have lived a complicated life...' He caught Kate's eyes in a silent plea for help.

'Aleksi isn't the settling down type,' Kate tried.

'I wasn't,' Aleksi corrected. 'Never did I consider marrying, and especially not being a parent.'

'Why?' The perpetual question came from Georgie, and Kate was glad for it.

'I did not think I would be very good at it,' Aleksi admitted. 'I was brought up to trust no one and I didn't— not anyone,' he elaborated, 'not even myself.' Georgie's tears had stopped. 'I see my brothers with their children and I wonder how they can be so sure they are doing the right thing by them, making the right decisions for them...'

He didn't know what else to say, so Kate stepped in then.

'Being a parent is a huge responsibility, Georgie, and Aleksi isn't sure…' She stopped as she felt his hand tighten on her shoulder.

'I'm not sure that I'll be the best father, but I will try…'

Kate could feel the blood pounding in her ears.

'I will do everything I can to look after you and your mother. I have a new brother, and I want to do the right thing by him too—but you, Georgie, and your mother come first. I will fight for what is mine—hopefully with honour.'

Georgie didn't understand, so Aleksi explained.

'Zakahr is my eldest brother—he has a right to the House of Kolovsky. But I will have a wife and daughter to look after…'

'We don't care about the money,' Georgie said. 'So long as we can have lots of channels on our television!'

'You deserve the very best in life.' Aleksi actually managed a smile as he spoke. 'And now I have someone to work for…' He did. All the years—the gambling, the searching, the reckless times—just melted away, because here before him was what really mattered.

'Us?' Georgie checked and Aleksi nodded.

'You two.'

'So I can tell the girls at school…'

'Tell them you are going to be a bridesmaid.'

Aleksi smiled, and Kate paled. 'You're supposed to ask *me* first.'

'Are you going to refuse?'

She looked at Georgie, and then at Aleksi, and then she looked into her own heart and she absolutely wouldn't dare refuse the gift she was staring at now— the gift of his love. There was, Kate realised, no greater love than that of a bad boy made good—it was there for the taking, a future with him, and all she had to do was say yes.

'I love you, Kate.'

He said it for the first time in front of Georgie—and Kate knew that he meant it. Because he might be reckless with his own heart at times, and even with hers, but always, always he had taken Georgie's welfare seriously—at the hospital, with her education. Always he had made sure that she was okay, and he wouldn't let her down now. So, whether he trusted himself or not, Kate did.

'Yuck,' Georgie said as it was sealed with a kiss.

'And now,' Aleksi said, quickly getting a handle on being a father, 'you can go to your room and play for a while.'

'I'm in my room.' Georgie pointed out.

So she was!

So they went to his.

'Ours,' he corrected, and then he thought of this house that was all tied up in Kolovsky. 'I will speak with Zakahr,' Aleksi promised. 'When I gave it all away I was only thinking of me...' She opened her mouth to speak, but he overrode her. 'You deserve something too.'

'I've got everything,' Kate said. 'I've never been more proud of you than when you handed it back to him. He's your brother.' She watched him screw up his eyes, and then he opened them again—to the woman who was going to be his wife. And he knew, finally knew, he could trust someone.

'Will you be there when I tell my mother?' Aleksi asked, and Kate didn't hesitate.

'I'll always be there.'

* * *

'She won't fit—there is not enough fabric…'

It had been Nina's response to the news of the wedding the following day. Her tears had soon dried and it was back to the pointed catty remarks as usual—this time about Kate's wedding dress.

And the planning for the wedding of the year had started in her next sentence!

The pleading too.

'Iosef is your twin—of course he must be your best man…'

'I love Iosef, but I have already discussed this with him.' Aleksi was pale—not that his mother noticed. Aleksi was bleeding inside now that the moment of truth had arrived. 'Iosef agrees this is the right thing to do—Zakahr is to be my best man.'

'Zakahr?' Nina frowned. '*Zakahr?* Why on earth would you choose a stranger? He's not even a colleague…'

'I thought he was your new best friend,' Aleksi taunted, 'as you've been singing his praises for months.'

'He helps with our charity. It is just business, Aleksi.'

'You really thought he liked you?' Aleksi said, gaining momentum now. 'You really thought he had the House of Kolovsky's best interests at heart?' He stared at his mother with utter contempt. 'You *fool*.'

'Don't you dare speak to me like that,' Nina retaliated. 'I am your mother!'

'And Zakahr is your *son*.'

Kate had never imagined she might feel sorry for Nina, never thought she could feel sympathy for a woman who had stood back and watched her son be beaten, who had denied him treatment for the sake of her reputation, who had abandoned her own flesh and blood in an orphanage and who had humiliated Kate at every turn. But watching the colour drain from Nina's well made-up face, watching her stumble, watching hands that, unlike her face, looked every bit her age hold onto the desk as her legs gave way, she felt sympathy override satisfaction and Kate found her a chair, helping Nina into it before she slipped to the floor.

'Riminic!' Nina sobbed the word out, and Kate realised then that she must have said it to herself every day.

'Remember Zakahr's words at your charity ball?' Aleksi was merciless. 'Remember how he prostituted himself to survive? How that boy, your son, was forced to beg, to steal, to…?'

'Stop!' It was Kate who halted him as Nina was gagging now. 'Aleksi, stop. She's heard enough.'

'She can't stand to hear it,' Aleksi said contemptuously. 'Zakahr *lived* it.'

'Forgive me!' Nina screamed, so loudly that even Lavinia came running, her bony legs struggling on six-inch heels as Nina sobbed louder. 'Forgive me, Aleksi.'

'It's not me who needs to forgive you,' Aleksi said. 'It's my brother—your son.'

'Leave it, Aleksi,' Kate said, and she was crying for both of them, for all of them, because there was no victory to be had here—just a whole lot of healing to take place.

So they left Lavinia comforting Nina, walked out of the golden doors and stood on the steps of Kolovsky as Aleksi took a deep breath, and then another one. The sun was shining and the world was waiting, and Kate knew they'd be okay because instead of walking on ahead Aleksi stopped and took her hand.

'Are you sure you want to be a Kolovsky?' he checked, and somehow, on the worst day, he made her laugh.

'Quite sure,' Kate assured him, and they looked over to the church across the road.

If they'd had a licence, she'd have married him there and then, but instead they walked over hand in hand and booked the date.

EPILOGUE

IT *was* the most beautiful dress in the world—at least it was to Kate.

As soft as petals it clung to her curves, and there was a hint of daring too.

It was a Kolovsky gown, but not *the* Kolovsky gown—because Kate didn't want it either.

'Do I look like a princess?' Georgie asked for the hundredth time as the Kolovsky dressers fussed with her mother.

'You do…' Kate said through chattering teeth, hardly able to stand the thought of so many eyes on her. It was more soothing to gaze at her daughter.

Her dress was simple yet stunning: silk, a shade pinker than her mother's. She had flowers on her head and her eyes were shining—clever and gifted, yes, but just a little girl who was dressed up today when, even better, all her little friends would see.

Even the one who had once pinched her!

Georgie's dress, though simple, was filled with tradition.

A new tradition—a new order.

Aleksi's gift to his new daughter had been jewels—jewels Georgie did not even know existed. They had been sewn into the hem of her dress. Jewels that would never see the light of day unless they were needed at some point in the future.

His way of saying that, come what might, with the House of Kolovsky, Aleksi's girls would always be safe.

It was a fairly low-key wedding, but that didn't stop the press clamouring—just who *was* Zakahr Belenki? Add to that the news that Nina Kolovsky was *resting* in a private hospital and might not make the wedding and it had them hanging from the trees.

But she made it.

Kate stood at the entrance to the church and was curiously proud of the woman she loathed.

A woman who stood tiny, shaky but straight, plastered in make-up, leaning a touch on Lavinia and trying very hard to smile.

Kate was proud of Nina's sons and daughter too.

Of Levander, who had flown his family from the UK... As she walked down the aisle she could see Dimitri smile and turn, and it made Kate smile too.

Of Iosef, who *was* Aleksi's best man—just not for today.

And Annika, who had looked out for Georgie in all of this.

She couldn't look at her husband-to-be as she walked, or she'd have started to cry—which she did when Zakahr turned around and nudged his new brother and smiled.

How did Zakahr do it?

How could he stand to be in the same room as all of them?

How did you start to forgive such betrayal?

And then she saw Aleksi, and nothing else mattered.

He kissed his bride, and then he did the nicest thing:

he went over and kissed a very proud Georgie before going back to Kate's side.

Back to his *krasavitsa*.

Coming Next Month

from **Harlequin Presents® EXTRA.** Available January 11, 2011.

#133 THE MAN BEHIND THE MASK
Maggie Cox
From Rags to Riches

#134 MASTER OF BELLA TERRA
Christina Hollis
From Rags to Riches

#135 CHAMPAGNE WITH A CELEBRITY
Kate Hardy
One Night at a Wedding

#136 FRONT PAGE AFFAIR
Mira Lyn Kelly
One Night at a Wedding

Coming Next Month

from **Harlequin Presents®.** Available January 25, 2011.

#2969 GISELLE'S CHOICE
Penny Jordan
The Parenti Dynasty

#2970 BELLA AND THE MERCILESS SHEIKH
Sarah Morgan
The Balfour Brides

#2971 HIS FORBIDDEN PASSION
Anne Mather

#2972 HIS MAJESTY'S CHILD
Sharon Kendrick

#2973 GRAY QUINN'S BABY
Susan Stephens
Men Without Mercy

#2974 HIRED BY HER HUSBAND
Anne McAllister

REQUEST YOUR
FREE BOOKS!

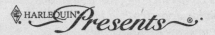

2 FREE NOVELS PLUS
2 FREE GIFTS!

YES! Please send me 2 FREE Harlequin Presents® novels and my 2 FREE gifts (gifts are worth about $10). After receiving them, if I don't wish to receive any more books, I can return the shipping statement marked "cancel." If I don't cancel, I will receive 6 brand-new novels every month and be billed just $4.05 per book in the U.S. or $4.74 per book in Canada. That's a saving of at least 15% off the cover price! It's quite a bargain! Shipping and handling is just 50¢ per book.* I understand that accepting the 2 free books and gifts places me under no obligation to buy anything. I can always return a shipment and cancel at any time. Even if I never buy another book, the two free books and gifts are mine to keep forever.

106/306 HDN E5M4

Name	(PLEASE PRINT)	

Address		Apt. #

City	State/Prov.	Zip/Postal Code

Signature (if under 18, a parent or guardian must sign)

Mail to the **Harlequin Reader Service:**
IN U.S.A.: P.O. Box 1867, Buffalo, NY 14240-1867
IN CANADA: P.O. Box 609, Fort Erie, Ontario L2A 5X3

Not valid for current subscribers to Harlequin Presents books.

Are you a current subscriber to Harlequin Presents books and want to receive the larger-print edition? Call 1-800-873-8635 today!

* Terms and prices subject to change without notice. Prices do not include applicable taxes. N.Y. residents add applicable sales tax. Canadian residents will be charged applicable provincial taxes and GST. Offer not valid in Quebec. This offer is limited to one order per household. All orders subject to approval. Credit or debit balances in a customer's account(s) may be offset by any other outstanding balance owed by or to the customer. Please allow 4 to 6 weeks for delivery. Offer available while quantities last.

Your Privacy: Harlequin Books is committed to protecting your privacy. Our Privacy Policy is available online at www.eHarlequin.com or upon request from the Reader Service. From time to time we make our lists of customers available to reputable third parties who may have a product or service of interest to you. If you would prefer we not share your name and address, please check here. ☐

Help us get it right—We strive for accurate, respectful and relevant communications. To clarify or modify your communication preferences, visit us at www.ReaderService.com/consumerchoice.

HP10R

*Harlequin Romance author Donna Alward is loved
for her gorgeous rancher heroes.*

*Meet Wyatt as he's confronted by both a precious
little pink bundle left on his doorstep and his neighbor Elli
who's going to show him the ropes....*

Introducing
PROUD RANCHER, PRECIOUS BUNDLE

THE SQUAWKING QUIETED as Elli picked the baby up, and
Wyatt turned around, trying hard to ignore the feelings of
inadequacy as Darcy immediately stopped fussing.

"Maybe she's uncomfortable. What do you think, sweet-
heart?" Elli turned her conversation to the baby.

"What do you think is wrong?" Wyatt asked, putting the
coffee pot back on the burner.

A strange look passed over Elli's face, one that looked
like guilt and panic. But it was gone quickly. "I couldn't
say," she replied.

"But you were so good with her this afternoon." Wyatt
put his hands on his hips.

"Lucky, that's all. I just...remembered a few things."
The same strange look flitted over her features once more.

Wyatt took the coffee to the table. "You fooled me. You
looked like you knew exactly what you were doing." So
much so that Wyatt had felt completely inept. A feeling he
despised. He was used to being the one in control.

Elli and Darcy walked the length of the kitchen and
back. After a few moments, she admitted, "I haven't really
cared for a baby before. The things I thought of were simply
things I'd heard about. Not from experience, Mr. Black."

Her chin jutted up, closing the subject but making him

want to ask the questions now pulsing through his mind. But then he remembered the old saying—*Don't look a gift horse in the mouth.* He'd benefit from whatever insight she had and be glad of it.

"I don't really know what babies need," he said. "I fed her, patted her back like you did, walked her to sleep, but every time I put her down…"

Wyatt almost groaned. Of course. He'd forgotten one important thing. He'd been so focused on getting the formula the right temperature that he'd forgotten to check her diaper. Not that he had any clue what to do there either.

Pulling calves and shoveling out stalls was far less intimidating than one tiny newborn.

"She's probably due for a diaper change, isn't she." He tried to sound nonchalant. This was a perfect opportunity. Elli must know how to change a diaper. He could simply watch her so he'd know better for the next time.

Instead, Elli came around the corner of the counter and placed Darcy back in his arms. "Here you go, Uncle Wyatt," she said lightly. "You get diaper duty. I'll fix the coffee. Cream and sugar?"

Oh boy, Wyatt thought, looking down into Darcy's pursed face, his smug plan blown to smithereens. He was in for it now.

Will sparks fly between Elli and Wyatt?

Find out in
PROUD RANCHER, PRECIOUS BUNDLE
Available February 2011 from Harlequin Romance

Try these Healthy and Delicious Spring Rolls!

INGREDIENTS

2 packages rice-paper spring roll wrappers (20 wrappers)

1 cup grated carrot

¼ cup bean sprouts

1 cucumber, julienned

1 red bell pepper, without stem and seeds, julienned

4 green onions finely chopped— use only the green part

DIRECTIONS

1. Soak one rice-paper wrapper in a large bowl of hot water until softened.

2. Place a pinch each of carrots, sprouts, cucumber, bell pepper and green onion on the wrapper toward the bottom third of the rice paper.

3. Fold ends in and roll tightly to enclose filling.

4. Repeat with remaining wrappers. Chill before serving.

Find this and many more delectable recipes including the perfect dipping sauce in

YOUR BEST BODY NOW

by

TOSCA RENO

WITH STACY BAKER

Bestselling Author of
THE EAT-CLEAN DIET®

Available wherever books are sold!